OUT OF THE PAST

Recent Titles by Christine Marion Fraser from Severn House

ULLIN MACBETH
WILD IS THE DAY

OUT OF THE PAST

Christine Marion Fraser

This first world edition published in Great Britain 1997 by
SEVERN HOUSE PUBLISHERS LTD of
9–15 High Street, Sutton, Surrey SM1 1DF.
This title first published in the U.S.A. 1998 by
SEVERN HOUSE PUBLISHERS INC of
595 Madison Avenue, New York, N.Y. 10022.

British Library Cataloguing in Publication Data

Fraser, Christine Marion

   Out of the past
   1.   Highlands (Scotland) – Fiction
   2.   Love stories
   I.   Title
   823.9'14 [F]

   ISBN 0 7278 5275 2

Typeset by Hewer Text Composition Services Limited,
Edinburgh, Scotland.
Printed and bound in Great Britain by
MPG Books Ltd, Bodmin, Cornwall.

Chapter One

"WELL, that's me packed and ready to go . . ."

Katrina lifted her suitcase from the chair and stood it beside a larger one she'd packed the previous evening. She paused and surveyed herself critically in the mirror. A too-pale face stared back at her and she sighed and pushed back her curtain of chestnut hair. "I look awful, as if I hadn't slept in ages."

Jilly sipped her coffee and surveyed her friend's face thoughtfully. "You haven't actually," she pointed out sympathetically. "The strain of the past few weeks are bound to show."

"Yes, I suppose so." Katrina's hazel eyes clouded. "It all seems unreal somehow. I suppose I haven't really taken in the fact that my mother is dead. I still wake in the night and fancy I hear her voice calling me."

Jilly ran a hand through her bouncy blonde hair, her pretty face unusually sober as she said slowly, "You'll get over it, Katie; it will take time, that's all. I think you've been absolutely wonderful and have nothing to reproach yourself for. You nursed your mum for nearly a year and it's natural for you to feel the world's a bit topsy-turvy at the moment."

1

Katrina sighed again. "That year seems like a lifetime. I wonder if I'll ever pick up the pieces again."

"Of course you will," Jilly said briskly. "When you return from Scotland and go back to the MoD you'll think you've never been away."

Katrina frowned in a distracted way. Just then she doubted very much if she could so easily slip back into her job as a secretary at the Ministry of Defence. It seemed aeons since her boss, Tony Adams, had assured her in his kindly way that he would keep her job open for her, no matter how long she had to be away. At the time, neither could have imagined just how long she'd be gone, but Tony, being the man he was, had proved to be very understanding about her mother's illness, and had recently assured her that her job was still there if she wanted it.

She knew she had no worries on that score, yet she was dreading going back. All the old memories of her relationship with Paul Carrington would be re-kindled and she was too drained both mentally and physically to take such painful memories . . .

Giving herself a little mental shake she dragged her mind away from Paul and, pulling on a colourful ski jacket, she paraded for Jilly's benefit. "Will I do?" she asked, a smile lighting her face as she walked round the room with an exaggerated swagger.

"You'll bowl 'em over," giggled Jilly. "You look as if you're dressed for the Arctic! The north of Scotland in winter! Better you than me. Still, all that mountain air ought to bring your colour back."

"I'm looking forward to it. I've always been fond of the country and with me being half Scottish the hills and

2

glens are in my blood. When I was a kid we had some wonderful holidays in Speyside and Dad always spoke of retiring back there. Mum loved it as much as he did and would have been quite happy living there, she would have thrown splendid ceilidhs and her door would have been constantly open to whoever came along."

"You might fall head over heels for some magnificent Scotsman and spend the rest of your days in the Scotch mist." Jilly sounded too optimistic to be teasing.

Katrina shook her head. "Hardly likely. I'm going for a rest, remember. I don't need an emotional entanglement at this stage in my life."

"Katie, you can't go moping over Paul Carrington all your life," said Jilly placidly. "As a man he was a dead loss anyway. The sea is full of other fish and it's high time you started angling."

Katrina experienced a recurring twinge of exasperation. She and Jilly had met at Secretarial College and joined the Ministry of Defence offices at the same time. They had known the same people, shared outings, shared clothes. But in the last year or so Katrina hadn't seen so much of her friend and discovered that during that time she'd expanded mentally whereas Jilly still remained as carefree and immature as a child.

She rarely took the trouble to delve into the deeper issues of life and at times her attitude could be annoying. She just didn't seem to realise that Katrina's affair with Paul had been much more than a casual one and couldn't be shrugged off so easily. As far as Katrina knew, Jilly had still to take a man seriously. She was the first to admit her various male admirers were just attractively packaged meal tickets who were as plentiful as they were varied. 'Still, she's only twenty-two,' Katrina thought indulgently, 'she's got plenty of time to get serious.'

It was with a nasty little shock that Katrina remembered she herself wouldn't be twenty-three till later that month. It proved how out of touch she had become. She felt years older than bubbly Jilly, to whom the latest shade of nail polish was more important than any man.

Katrina looked affectionately at her friend, still attired in her baggy wrap and Snoopy mules, her blonde hair attractively mussed round her fresh face. Normally she slept till midday on Saturdays, but on this occasion she'd made a heroic effort to rouse herself at seven so that she could say goodbye.

For two weeks now, Katrina had shared Jilly's tiny flat, which consisted of a bedroom, living room, kitchenette and bathroom. Katrina had brought some things from her mother's house in Hampstead, a sofa bed had been installed in the bedroom, and in it she spent sleepless nights going over in her mind half-formed plans for her future.

The house in Hampstead where she had lived most of her life was in the hands of lawyers, and if it was sold when she returned from her month-long stay in Scotland she intended to use some of the proceeds to purchase a flat and bank the remainder 'for a rainy day'.

She'd inherited a practical outlook from her father, together with his marvellous sense of humour. Her deep hazel eyes were his and so too was her small, straight nose with its attractive sprinkling of freckles. But her mane of chestnut hair and wide sensitive mouth had come from her mother whose sweet and buoyant nature had ensured her popularity with everyone she met.

They had been a happy and close-knit family but tragedy struck when James Cameron died soon after being involved in a serious road accident. Katrina was just fifteen when it happened and she thought her world had ended with her father's death. Her mother had never been the same afterwards, she hadn't smiled nearly so much; she didn't laugh as she used to or invite friends round to the house as she had done when her husband was alive. It was as if a lamp had been dimmed inside of her, never to glow with such brilliance again.

James Cameron's well-paid position with a firm of architects had meant a comfortable lifestyle for his wife and daughter and he'd provided well for them after his death. Katrina had never wanted for anything but now, with her mother gone after a long and painful illness, she felt she wanted for everything that meant anything in the world to her.

Jilly had been wonderful all along and insisted she stay at her flat till she got settled. Normally her tidy mind would have rebelled at the disorderly chaos around her but she was too dazed just now to care and allowed herself to sink gratefully into Jilly's untidy, unconventional world.

During the day she tried to keep herself as busy as possible, and had little time to mope in the evenings when streams of Jilly's acquaintances drifted into the flat at odd hours to drape themselves over the furniture and pluck at musical instruments. But the night hours dragged by and though her doctor had prescribed sleeping pills she stubbornly refused to allow them to become a habit and had stopped taking them after the first few nights.

Jilly yawned widely and put her drained coffee cup on the dressing table. "I'm dead. Joe's party was wild. Jake poured beer into Sam's trumpet and they had a go at each other in the hall while the rest of us danced in the living room. I didn't get in till three. If I can find my bed I'm going back as soon as you've gone."

Katrina threw a laughing glance at the litter of clothes by her friend's bedside. "At least my room at Balgower Farm won't look like a street market, yet – if my memory serves me well – Belle Grant was never too fussy either. Homely and comfortable might be an adequate description of the farmhouse."

"So your father's cousin isn't terribly fogy-ish?"

"Lord no! I remember as a kid thinking it was a bit of a madhouse with hens roosting in the trees and eggs dropping from the heavens so to speak."

Jilly choked with laughter. "Sounds as if things won't be dull anyway."

"They never were at the farm," said Katrina dreamily. "I'll pop over to see Peggy while I'm there."

"Oh yes, Preggie Peggy. How many at the last count?"

"Two, a little girl of eighteen months and a new baby."

Jilly grimaced. "Not bad going for someone married just two and a half years."

"Peggy always wanted children. She loved them, even when she was just a kid herself."

Jilly examined her nails. "Hmm, with some women

it's an ambition. Only a scatterbrain like Peggy could manage to get knocked down in a London street by an up-and-coming Scots doctor and on his subsequent visits to see her in hospital wangle a marriage proposal. It's not as if she's a looker."

"Looks aren't everything," said Katrina rather sharply, rising to the defence of Margaret Melville whom she had known since schooldays and who had been more a friend to her than anyone else she knew, even Jilly. "Peggy's a very sweet person and she's got bags of personality."

Jilly's grin was unrepentant. "Looks mean a lot in my book – I'd never have gotten anywhere without them. Let's face it, Peggy had to grab at her chances; with looks you can have a bit of fun before taking the plunge."

The bell went. "My taxi." Katrina picked up her cases.

"Hey, kid!" Jilly hugged her friend. "Have a good time. Bring me back a kilted Scot – preferably rich. Ring often – reverse the charges if you have to. Joe helps me with the bill because I allow him to practise his trumpet here at the risk of getting thrown out. You can let me know if those Scottish New Years are fact or myth."

"I'll do that." Katrina went to the door.

"Katie, just a minute," Jilly's voice was anxious. "There ought to be a few parties over Christmas and I can't afford anything new. Could I borrow your red dress – your blue trouser suit, too? I promise not to spoil them."

"Help yourself, what's left in the wardrobe is yours till I get back."

"You're a pal." Jilly wandered back to the bedroom,

7

saying over her shoulder, "Have a safe journey. If you must talk to strange men make sure they're loaded. A millionaire wouldn't go amiss, especially if he's young and good-looking. Just the thing to cheer you up."

Sitting in the taxi to Euston, Katrina recalled her friend's nonsense with an indulgent smile though she was also niggled by the constant hints that she ought to get fixed up with a male companion. Girls like Jilly assumed that life was incomplete unless it contained a stream of fun-loving men, and she had a knack of making Katrina feel in some way inadequate.

She sighed and gazed out at the London streets, a part of her wishing that she could be a bit more like Jilly, able to take all sorts of frivolous relationships in her stride; to let all her emotions ride on the surface, never to let them get deep enough to bruise and leave scars. Yet hadn't she once been rather like Jilly? Enjoying the attention of boys, giggling, flirting? Playing the field? During her final years at school there had been lots of healthy, normal relationships with boys and when she had progressed to college there had been others, a little more serious, more intense, more searching.

When she later secured a job with the Ministry of Defence, life had seemed perfect. The illusion further heightened a year later when Paul Carrington joined the department. He was handsome, charming, witty and he'd been around, that much was obvious from his assured, sophisticated manner.

She had been entranced by him from the start and was stunned when it became clear he was interested in her and after a while had invited her out. She remembered the envy of the other girls, Jilly's laughing, teasing remarks.

She would have been lying if she hadn't admitted to feeling flattered and special. Paul had been a young girl's dream materialised into flesh and blood. He had wined and dined her at expensive restaurants and she had fully imagined herself to be in love with him. But all too soon the real Paul had emerged. She had discovered the kind of man he was under that polished veneer and all her dreams had been shattered like fragile glass . . .

Chapter Two

THE taxi came to a halt and she forgot Paul in the flurry of getting herself through the crowds in the station. She breathed a sigh of relief when at last she was settled in her seat on the train. Ideally she would have liked to fly but until the Hampstead house was sold and the estate tidied up she couldn't afford to indulge in too much expense.

Feeling the compartment stuffy, she got up to stow her jacket in the luggage rack. Her tight-fitting top clung to her petite figure and she was aware of several admiring glances thrown in her direction from males in the nearby vicinity. She blushed a little as a warm glow spread through her. She had almost forgotten how good it felt to be on the receiving end of manly appreciation and she realised again just how out of touch she was with things that other girls took for granted. It was like emerging afresh from childhood into adolescence, unsure, wary, sensitive to each small reaction of the opposite sex.

Well, she wasn't exactly as naïve as that. After her experiences with Paul she could hardly have emerged unscathed. In fact she was a little wiser, certainly more cynical, and though she had built a protective and occasionally defensive shell around herself it was a fragile one and as liable to shatter as an eggshell.

She was still vulnerable and that was why she was determined not to allow herself to become serious about a man for a long time to come. If the occasional light-hearted adventure came her way she most certainly wouldn't turn her back on it. Despite Paul, she enjoyed the company of men but allow herself to become emotionally involved she would not.

The man in the seat opposite had nice hands. She studied them as they lay folded in repose over his briefcase. Paul's hands were like that: fine yet strong, the fingers long and sensitive, the nails short and clean. With hands like that she had expected his touch to be gentle but it had been the exact opposite.

Crude would be a more apt description of his sexual advances. There had been no tenderness, no loveplay, nothing but a harsh attempt to make her submit. She could still see the sweat gleaming on his face as she fought him, still hear his enraged oaths as she tore herself free of his fierce embraces.

'What's wrong with you, Katie?' he had asked her once. 'You know you want it as much as I do, why don't you just give in and then we'll all be happy?'

'Not like this, Paul,' she had answered steadily. 'I don't like being mauled around like a rag doll with no feelings. Try treating me like a human being and then I might behave like one.'

'Oh, so you want the romantic bit, eh? Sweet nothings in your ear, a goodnight kiss with no strings attached?'

'Don't be silly, that's not what I meant, though a little bit of that would be no bad thing. Every girl likes to be treated like a lady now and then and someday I hope you'll find out what I mean.'

He hadn't taken her seriously yet she had continued to see him, had gone on hoping that he liked her for herself and not what he could get from her. She had ignored the rumours that he was a womaniser, that before her there had been strings of others.

According to what she heard she had been his most enduring relationship and it was later, when she saw him in a clearer light, that she understood why. She had remained unconquered. If he had set about trying to win her with more tenderness it would have been different. She had wanted him but he didn't know how to go about arousing a woman and he had left her cold.

Her affair with him had gone on for six months before the final, hurtful end. Her strong, determined, lovely mother was ill and not strong anymore. Katrina had decided to leave her job and nurse her mother herself. There hadn't been enough hours in the day to do all the things she had to and there had been little time left over for any sort of social life.

Paul hadn't liked this one bit. 'What about us, Katie?' he had said, peevishly. 'When am I going to see you properly again? I'm sorry about your mother, of course I am, but surely you could get somebody else in to look after her? She would understand, she isn't a selfish person.'

'No, but you are,' Katrina had flashed back. 'You're only thinking of yourself, not me, not my mother. It's me she needs and it's me who'll be looking after her. That's how it's going to be, take it or leave it, and if you thought anything of me you'd stand by and support me with everything you've got.'

Soon after that he had left her. The bubble had finally

burst. When she most needed him he had turned his back on her and later she heard there was somebody else. He had also secured the promotion he'd always wanted and was abroad a lot on Government business. His horizons were broadening while hers were narrowing. That had been nine months ago and she hadn't seen him since, though even now it still hurt to think about him and how easily he had been able to let her go.

The train rushed on and she shook herself angrily, forcing her thoughts away from Paul. It was an episode in her life that was over and done with and she had to forget. She half thought of going to the buffet carriage but she wasn't very hungry. The motion of the train was making her sleepy.

Drowsily she thought of her father's cousin, Belle Grant, and a smile lifted her mouth. Belle and her husband Bob had come south for her mother's funeral. Bob was dour, yet thoughtful and kind. Belle was talkative, cheerful and motherly in a sympathetic but non-smothering fashion. 'Of course you must come and spend a few weeks with us, Katrina,' she had said firmly. 'Take in Christmas and the New Year. It will help you get over the first month or so. You can sit back and take things easy, plan out your future in the peace and quiet of the country.'

The train got into Glasgow Central just before lunchtime and she had something to eat in the station buffet before getting a taxi to Queen Street to catch the Inverness train.

The journey north passed pleasantly, and she watched entranced as the countryside unfolded before her: the

14

bare winter fields, great shaggy stretches of moorland, the peaks of hills hidden by cloud, tiny crofthouses snuggling into the hollows beneath.

The mood changed as the train sped its way into the Highlands, the snow-capped bens were more majestic and brooding; the rushing burns glinted in the corries. Rivers and glens, panoramic views; great stretching vistas sailed past her vision and a feeling of excitement surged within her.

This was it, the Highlands of Scotland! She was coming back! After all these years she was seeing it again and a memory came to her of that last holiday here. Long summer days when the sky had never grown dark; fishing in the river with her father, paddling in the trout burns; walking with her mother through woodlands filled with wild flowers; helping Bob on the farm, Belle in the kitchen; laughter, talk; the big snuggly feather bed with her mother coming to tuck her in and tell her a story she made up as she went along.

It had been good, so good. When she remembered those days they had been like little cameos in her mind and she always hoped they'd go back. But somehow the months, years, had slipped by and they had been too busy. Her father's job seemed to take up more of his time; she had school, holidays with friends, had gone abroad with her parents. Her mother had entertained more; there were never enough hours in the day to do all the things they wanted to do.

They had, of course, kept in touch with the Grants: Christmas cards, letters, phonecalls. 'We will go back someday,' James Cameron had often said. 'I'd like to retire to the north, it's a nice life they have up there.

A slower pace than here; there's room to think and see things in a better perspective.'

And now it was too late, her parents were gone, she was returning to Scotland without them. Regrets flooded her being. She sat back in her seat and felt a prickle of tears behind her lids. Dashing them away she told herself not to be silly, it was no use dwelling on the past; *now* was what mattered and she had to make the most of it. Her mother would have been the first to tell her so. 'Think positive.' Laura Cameron had made that her own adage and quoted it to her daughter whenever she had been down in the dumps.

All right, Mum, I'll try, Katrina thought with a smile, *only you'll have to remind me now and again because this is all a bit daunting without you and Dad.*

Dusk was settling over the countryside and closing her eyes she gave herself up to her thoughts as the train sped on to its destination.

Bob knew the time of her arrival at Inverness and he was there on the platform to meet her. With old-fashioned courtesy he removed his cap and extended his hand to take hers firmly. He was a stockily built man with a shy smile, a brown, weatherbeaten face, and a habit of rubbing his stubbly chin when he was speaking. The big hands that grasped her suitcases were reassuringly strong and capable and she felt immediately at ease as she walked along beside him.

"It's nice to see you, lass," he nodded, leading the way out of the station to an ancient Morris Traveller which had blobs of red lead on its wings to cover up the patches of rust.

As he was loading her luggage he asked about her journey from the south. His voice was as slow and firm as his handshake had been. Her memories of him were astonishingly vivid and she thought how little he had changed over the years. At her mother's funeral she had been too numb to take in the people around her but now she was able to see him in a clearer light and to appreciate his sincerity and kindness.

She had been ten years old the last time she had come to spend a holiday with Belle and Bob, but it might well have been yesterday. The years rolled away as she climbed into the car. As a little girl she had ridden in a similar one through the glens of Speyside, crushed in beside other children from neighbouring farms. On one memorable occasion she had accompanied Bob on a trip to the cattle market and she had made the return journey snuggled close to a black and white calf with big mournful eyes and a huge tongue which had licked everything in sight, including her hands and knees.

Darkness had fallen and the lights of Inverness were twinkling. Katrina settled back in her seat to listen as Bob talked about the small changes that had taken place in the locality, mostly concerning country matters: people that had died, others who had married, those that had grown up and left, some that had come back. Many of these were vague in Katrina's memory but the names were familiar since Speyside was full of Grants, Camerons, Frasers and MacAuleys.

He also spoke about the effects of BSE on farming in general but on a brighter note was able to say that his stock had been given the 'BSE free' tag, as had other farms in the area, and that things

were ticking along and they would all get by somehow.

It seemed no time at all till they were turning off the
main road and rattling up the rutted track to Balgower
Farm. The farmhouse was a big, solid building huddled
under the lea of the hills. Fields stretched on either side,
the deep, dark waters of a lochan lapped the banks of a
birch wood on the western side of the farm buildings.

Bob brought the car to a shuddering halt and it was
immediately surrounded by three excited sheepdogs,
barking and wagging their tails. Katrina felt a shaft
of pleasure go through her. Almost thirteen years had
elapsed since she was last here, yet it was all just the
same. Automatically, she peered through the window
to the straggle of sturdy sycamores that gave the house
shelter from the wind. The lights from the house lit up
the trees. Sure enough, one or two hens were roosting on
the lower branches, a few more cocked inquisitive eyes
from the remains of an old car on the edge of a field.

A wide beam of light flooded the gravel drive as the
door was thrown open and Belle Grant came rushing out
to hug Katrina and lead her inside. Belle was a well-built
woman of fifty with lively brown eyes set in a round, sweet
face. She was dressed in a fawn Fair Isle jumper and a
brown tweed skirt which was coming away slightly at
the hem. There was something about her that reminded
Katrina of her father. Her voice was very pleasant to the
ears with its Highland burr and Katrina felt immediately
at home as the older woman helped her to remove her
jacket and made her sit down on a comfortable chair.

The kitchen was warm and homely with its well-used,

deep armchairs and oak sideboard, the top of which brimmed with knick-knacks and photographs. There was one of Katrina as a little girl standing in a field holding a pony by its bridle. Beside it was one of her parents sitting together on a bench outside Balgower Farm. Three cats were piled on a handmade rag rug in front of the ancient Aga stove set into a red-tiled alcove. The fragrance of newly baked bread and homemade broth filled Katrina's nostrils and all at once she felt very hungry.

"There now," beamed Belle Grant, "you sit there and get nice and comfy. I expect you must be starving and from the look of you, you need some fattening up. You're also far too pale, Katrina, but don't worry, a few weeks in our good Scottish air should see the roses back in your cheeks . . ." She paused. "There I go, Bob says I go yapping on like one of the dogs. Of course you're pale, you've been through a lot. I just hope you'll be happy here and won't be bored."

Katrina smiled. "I won't get bored – Belle. You don't mind if I call you that, do you? Cousin Belle seems so formal now that I'm grown-up."

Belle was delighted at the suggestion. She hummed happily under her breath as she set about putting the finishing touches to the table. Bob came in with Katrina's cases and was directed to take them upstairs. "Away you go up with him, Katrina," instructed Belle with a smile. "Make sure he doesn't put them in the wrong room. It's at the end of the passage. The same one you slept in when you were a wee lassie."

Katrina looked around her affectionately as she followed Bob into her room. It was delightful with

19

its camped ceiling, rose-sprigged wallpaper, and fresh white paint. "I hope you didn't do this especially for me, Bob?" she said, anxiously.

"Ach well, it was needing done anyway," Bob said with a shrug of his big shoulders. His eyes twinkled. "To tell the truth, Belle nagged me so much about getting things to rights for you coming I was glad to come up here for a bit of peace. She isn't the sort to nag as a rule and never over-fussy about the house but she was that looking forward to you being here she wanted things done she's never bothered about before."

He went off smiling and Katrina flopped down on the big feather bed to bounce herself with pleasure as she had done as a child. Rummaging in her bag she found her comb and got up to run it through her thick tresses. The eyes that looked back at her from the mirror were brighter than they had been; she just knew that this holiday at Balgower Farm was going to be the best thing that had happened to her for ages . . .

"Dinner's ready!" Belle's lusty call came from below and with a chuckle Katrina ran quickly to the bathroom to wash her hands. Inwardly she groaned when she saw the laden table prepared by Belle but surprised herself by eating an enormous meal of steak and kidney pie followed by apple tart smothered in fresh cream.

Afterwards, when she had helped Belle clear away and wash up, she sat curled up in a deep armchair, listening to Belle and Bob chattering. When she could keep her eyes open no longer Belle escorted her upstairs to the bathroom where fresh towels were laid and a steaming bath had been run. "Into that, lassie, it will help you to relax and get a good night's sleep. First night in a strange bed can be a bit harrowing."

But somehow Katrina felt that her first night at Balgower Farm wasn't going to be in the least harrowing, especially when, after soaking for a blissful twenty minutes, she went to her room to find the patchwork quilt turned down and her blue cotton nightdress rolled snugly round a hot-water bag.

Wriggling out of her wrap she slipped into the deliciously warm nightdress and got into bed. It was like floating on a big, fluffy cloud. Snuggling into her pillows she gazed around her with pleasure then snapped out the bedside light. It was very quiet and peaceful. Nothing disturbed the stillness of the countryside. The city and all its memories seemed a million miles away. Jilly wouldn't like it here, that was for sure. She had often declared that the quiet of country nights frightened her to death and she needed the hum of traffic to lull her to sleep. I'll give her a ring tomorrow, thought Katrina, sleepily. She pulled one of the pillows down and cuddled it to her breast, feeling like the contented child of long ago who had hugged her dolls in this very same bed. If nothing else, this was going to be a peaceful holiday, a brief respite in which she could gather her thoughts and prepare herself for her future. It would be strange going back to work at the MoD. For almost a year her life had revolved round her mother and much of her time had been spent within the four walls of the house in Hampstead. She supposed in time she would get used to living alone in a flat in the city.

Alone! A slight panic rose in her. She didn't want

always to be alone. One day she might find someone to share her life . . . if only Paul had been different . . . She pushed Paul away and drifted off on the warm, fluffy cloud that held her and lulled her senses.

Chapter Three

KATRINA spent the next morning familiarising herself
with her surroundings. Balgower Farm was a fine,
big place, full of nooks and crannies and numerous
outbuildings; hens and geese strutted, pigs snorted, cats
lurked in dark corners and stared at her as she poked
about in the sheds, and it was lovely to go into the
warm, steamy atmosphere of the byre where the cows
munched hay and looked at her with their big, placid
long-lashed eyes.

So rewarding, seeing it all, reliving the memories of
childhood, yet thinking that in some subtle way it
had changed, not as vast as she had once thought
but better for all that, cosier and more homely than
ever. And somehow she noticed the surrounding scenery
more: the fields and farmlands stretching away to that
breathtaking vista of blue hills, the sparkling rivers,
the silver birches dotted everywhere, acres and acres of
wild moorland spread over the landscape like a russet
blanket.

In the course of her wanders she spoke to one or two
farmhands, in particular Jacky Grainger, a red-haired,
muscular young man who was only too willing to fill
her in with details about the running of the farm and

to refresh her memory about the names of local people she had half-forgotten.

"I think I remember you," she told him at one point. "You came from the village and used to come with us when Bob took us on outings."

"That's right," he said, eagerly. "Now I'm all grown-up and have to work for a living but I like it here, and get on well with Bob and Belle."

They conversed pleasantly for a little while longer. When she said she had to be on her way he stood watching her appreciatively till she disappeared from view.

"I see you've been reacquainting yourself with old friends," Belle greeted Katrina when at last she went indoors at lunchtime. "I saw you talking to Jacky. He's a nice lad and a willing worker and I'm sure he'll be only too happy to keep you company whenever you feel like it. He has a girlfriend, but they argue a bit, and sometimes I think that Jacky hasn't played the field enough – if you see what I mean."

There was a gleam in Belle's eye as she spoke and Katrina had to hide a smile. "Oh, yes, Jacky Grainger, he was telling me about the neighbours and the things that some of them have achieved."

"Ay, we have our share of clever folk hereabouts," Belle paused in the act of opening the oven door and her face took on an animated expression that Katrina was fast getting to know. "Take Laurence Sinclair, for example, he's a well-known novelist now, his books are bestsellers and he's always being invited to appear on TV chat shows."

"Laurence Sinclair," Katrina said, musingly. "I can't

recall seeing anyone of that name on TV, though I haven't watched much of that recently. I was too busy with Mum to have time for anything else."

"Ach well, to us he's just Larry Sinclair, local lad turned author. You might remember him if you saw him, he was born and bred here; a tall, fair boy who used to help Bob with the harvest. He lived with his sister and his great aunt at Dalmuir Croft.'

Katrina laughed. "It's a bit much, trying to take in the names of everyone and where they live, it will probably all come back but right now I'm enjoying just being here with you and Bob, talking of whom, here he comes now, looking as hungry as a hunter."

Belle gave a yelp and opened the oven door to withdraw a shepherd's pie just as Bob came in, sniffing the air, rubbing his hands in anticipation of the forthcoming meal, and Larry Sinclair was forgotten in the bustle of serving lunch.

"Belle, who is that man? I've a feeling I've seen him before somewhere." Katrina tried to sound casual as she lifted her glass of dry martini to her lips. She was sitting with Belle and Bob in the lounge bar of the Cairngorm Inn which nestled on the fringes of a spruce forest just outside the village of Nethy.

She had enjoyed her day pottering about the farm and would have been quite happy to spend a second evening just chatting to her hosts in the cosy farm-house kitchen. But Belle had suggested they all go out for a drink, and though Katrina suspected the outing was for her benefit and not because it was Belle's habit to go socialising, she agreed and they had rattled the two miles to the hotel in the Morris Traveller.

Belle had said it would be reasonably quiet at this time of year, but even so there were a fair number of people sipping drinks in the lounge. Most of them were locals but there was a group of rather noisy tourists dressed in baggy wool jerseys and woollen hats. Every minute or so they erupted into gales of laughter as they loudly recreated some adventure they had enjoyed on the Cairngorms ski slopes.

The atmosphere of the room was lively and cosy; brasses of all descriptions hung above the bar in the corner, and a log fire crackled in the hearth of a stone fireplace. Katrina quickly shed her jacket, glad that she had opted to wear a blouse instead of a sweater.

At Katrina's question Belle was immediately alert; her eyes raked the room and almost at once a smile lit her face. "Oh, it's Larry, Larry Sinclair, the lad I was telling you about earlier. So, you remember him, after all, Katrina? I thought you might if you saw him again."

Katrina drew in her breath, her eyes strayed once more to the big, fair man over by the fire. He was in conversation with some other men, his face glowing, and his deep laugh rang out frequently. It wasn't that how-ever which had made Katrina notice him. His physical attributes were obvious but he had something else that singled him out from the crowd: an aura of magnetism emanated from every inch of him, drawing eyes across the room. Several girls were doing their best to attract his attention but he was engrossed in conversation with Jacky Grainger whom Katrina had met that afternoon.

The handsome, lean face of Larry Sinclair stirred

memories in Katrina. Now that she had seen him she remembered him coming to Balgower Farm. He'd seemed almost grown-up to her then, though he must only have been sixteen or so. Certain things had stuck in her mind: his teasing, that annoying habit he had of pulling her ponytail and calling her 'a little witch'. He glanced up suddenly and his gaze alighted directly on her. She quickly dropped her eyes, feeling foolish at having been caught watching a man who, though not a complete stranger to her, was certainly no close friend either.

His conversation with Jacky over, he excused himself and crossing the room he came straight over to where she was sitting with Bob and Belle. Bob was rising to his feet, smiling with pleasure as he took Larry's hand and shook it heartily. "Well then, Larry, how are you? I'm glad you came over to say hello. We have Belle's cousin staying with us, Katrina Cameron, maybe you remember her? She used to come to Balgower for holidays and was there when you helped us with the harvest."

"Och, Bob," Belle chimed in, "that's no way to introduce two people who haven't met in years, you have to do it right or not at all . . ."

Larry grinned and held up a protesting hand. "Informal's good enough for me, Belle." His gaze fell on Katrina and she was annoyed to feel herself flushing. "I think I do remember you. You were a skinny little kid with a ponytail and freckles and you liked to be called Katie because you thought Katrina was too stuck up. Hi, there, Katie, I'm Larry Sinclair in case you've forgotten and I'm pleased to make your acquaintance

27

again." Hastily she took his proffered hand and let it go almost immediately.

"What will you have to drink, Larry?" Bob asked.

"I was just going to ask you the same question. It's the least I can do to compensate for not taking a run over to see you. I've been so busy since I got back, I'm leading the life of a recluse. You take whisky, don't you, on the rocks, and I can see you're on the orange juice, Belle."

"I'm driving back," she said, ruefully. "Someone has to stay sober and this time that someone is me."

"I'm in the same boat," he laughed, then turning to Katrina who was making a show of rummaging through her bag he went on, "What about you, Katie? I'm sure you could manage another one of those."

Katrina shook her head. "I won't have anything else, Mr Sinclair, but thank you anyway." She hated herself for sounding so unbearably polite, also at quavering out the words too breathlessly. Impatiently, she set her bag aside and looked up into eyes that were a deep blue, so hard and piercing in their directness she was mesmerised. Certain facts filtered into her mind, one of them being that he was tall enough to make her strain her neck to look up at him and that his fair hair was a startling contrast to the tanned skin of his strong face which was softened slightly by a cleft in his chin.

He was wearing casual clothes and looked very relaxed as he stood there, though at her words his mouth quirked into a rather amused smile. "Can I ask, do you remember me from away back? Or have you been talking?"

Belle clicked her tongue. "Of course we've been talking – or rather I have. When we came in Katrina said she thought she knew you and of course, in a way she does, though she's never seen you on TV and doesn't know a great deal about your books."

"Really?" His amusement was genuine now. "That makes a change. It also cuts me down to size . . ." His gaze lingered on Katrina's face. "It's all coming back; how annoyed you used to get when I teased you about your freckles, the day you fell in the yard and skinned your knees but wouldn't cry in case I thought you were soft. Oh, yes, Katie. I do remember you, though I must confess I've had my memory jogged over the years by Belle, who kept me posted about your progress since you grew up."

His eyes flicked over Katrina in a swift appraisal, lingering for a few moments on her breasts which rose softly against the silk material of her blouse, before travelling up once more to her face. "If you don't mind me saying so," he said softly, "the years have made a big improvement. You can tell me later what you think of me. It might be something I don't want to hear in front of my friends."

He moved away to get the drinks and Belle looked at Katrina. "Well, what do you think? He's a lovely man, isn't he, yet he's never let his fame go to his head and fits in here as good as anybody else."

"I thought he was a bit too confident and he can certainly turn on the charm; he also gave me the impression that he thinks he's God's gift to women."

"It's just his way," said Belle soothingly. She gave Katrina a sidelong glance. "Some people might say he's a bit too big for his boots but they're maybe just envious because he's done so well for himself. He is a bit of a celebrity after all and he's popular with women – they don't run after him, they chase him."

Katrina tilted her chestnut head. "I won't be one of them," she declared with conviction. "I wouldn't give him the satisfaction." She saw the twinkle in the older woman's eyes and allowed herself to relax a little. "He *is* good-looking," she conceded, "and that tan . . . he didn't get it here, surely?"

"He's been in Australia. Joan, his sister, emigrated some years ago and he hops over there whenever he can. He does a lot of travelling but he always comes back here to write his books. When his great aunt died he bought a cottage a mile or two from Aviemore where he can work in peace."

Jacky Grainger came over, a smile spreading across his smooth-skinned face. "Nice to see you again, Katrina," he nodded. "Can I get you something to drink?"

Earlier in the day Jacky had made it plain that he found Katrina attractive and she returned his smile. He was nice, pleasant and eager to please. She hesitated. If she accepted his offer he would come and sit beside her which would exclude Larry Sinclair from the scene and though one half of her didn't want that, the other half warned her that to get to know him better might not be wise. She had barely spoken to him, yet already he invaded her senses so much she felt distracted by him.

The arrival of a pretty, dark-haired girl took the decision out of her hands. The newcomer wound her arm through Jacky's and smiled charmingly at Katrina. Jacky smiled ruefully as he introduced her. "This is Elaine – my fiancée. We're being married in the spring which she thinks gives her the right to watch me like a hawk."

"It does," Elaine chided, gently but firmly, though her smiling eyes were still on Katrina. "He's making the most of his freedom and fancies himself as the local Romeo at the moment."

Point taken, thought Katrina, as Jacky was led firmly away.

Chapter Four

LARRY SINCLAIR was coming back. The lounge was growing smoky and his head was a bright beacon under the hazy lights. He set the drinks down and without preliminaries folded his lean frame into the space at Katrina's side, forcing her to move along the seat in order to keep some distance between them.

"Cheers." His long fingers closed round the glass of lemonade shandy he had bought for himself and, raising it to his lips, he took a long draught after which he settled himself more comfortably, sliding one arm across the back of Katrina's seat in a gesture that was oddly intimate though was possibly done in all innocence. Yet when she glanced at him and saw a gleam of laughter in his eyes she wasn't so sure. "Now tell me," he drawled laconically, "why have you stayed away for so long? If my memory serves me well you were just a little kid last time you were in these parts."

Choosing to ignore his last words she answered off-handedly. "I always wanted to come back but somehow we never quite made it; my parents were busy. I was occupied with school and went away to summer camps and trips to Europe. Dad and Mum wanted to travel and we began going abroad for our family holidays, mostly France but sometimes we had a winter break in Switzerland."

He let out his breath with a hiss. "Switzerland? You only had to come across the border to find mountains and snow. We're known as Ski Valley now. I take it you learned to ski abroad?"

"Only just," she said, modestly, but Belle leaned over and said enthusiastically,

"Her mother used to write and tell me that Katrina took to skiing like a duck to water."

"Hmm," he murmured thoughtfully. "Pity the best runs are incomplete at the moment. We might have made a good team – still, there's always the artificial ski slopes at the Aviemore Centre."

His blue gaze had fastened on her mouth and in confusion she said quickly, "It's so long ago now. I'm out of practice and anyway . . ."

"You wouldn't like to go anywhere with a man you've only just met," he interposed coolly and she turned away quickly from his searching gaze. His knee brushed against hers and she shivered as if he had touched her naked flesh. He was so big and powerful sitting there beside her she was overwhelmed by him and wished he would move away.

She felt small and vulnerable and terribly nervous. She shook herself angrily and forced herself to behave normally. The room had grown stuffy. She felt warm, too warm, and the fact didn't entirely owe itself to the heat in the room. She could no longer recognise the individual voices of the people in close proximity. They mingled into an annoying throb that beat inside her head.

"I was sorry to hear about your mother." His cool,

deep tones broke into her confused mind like a pebble dropping into a pool of water. "I remember her quite well; she used to tell stories, just made them up as she went along, and one day, when we were all sitting in the barn, drinking lemonade and listening to her, I thought about showing her some of the things I'd written down and she encouraged me to carry on. I'd never shown my jottings to anyone else before. She was the first, and I've never forgotten the influence she had on my future as a writer."

Katrina's throat tightened. "I didn't know. Perhaps I was too young to take notice. Mum was like that though, bucking people up, persuading them to keep going when they felt low. But how did you know she had died? You said you hadn't been over to see Belle and Bob."

"Highland telegraph." His hand stirred at her back and his thumb touched the top of her spine. Accident or purpose? She couldn't be sure. "And as I told you," he went on, "Belle kept me informed about you and your family. She enjoyed getting the letters your father wrote and would tell me little snippets of news."

She leaned forward and lifted her glass to her lips, glad that her hair had fallen forward to hide her flaming cheeks. His left hand came forward to lift away the gleaming chestnut strands. His index finger caressed her jawline. Belle and Bob were occupied with some people they knew and Katrina felt obliged to stay right where she was and somehow keep up a conversation with Larry Sinclair.

He seemed to know all about her and she remembered that he had been talking to Jacky. Talking about her? No! She shrugged the notion away. It was too preposterous for words. Why would a man like Larry Sinclair while away his time talking about a girl he barely knew?

His face came closer to hers and her indrawn breath didn't escape his notice. "Little witch," he murmured playfully. "All grown-up now, aren't you? And if I may say so, you've blossomed in all the right places . . ."

She turned an angry face. "You may *not* say so, Mr Sinclair – and – please – I'd rather you kept your hands to yourself!"

"Why? I think you're enjoying this as much as I am. Why don't we put it to a test? Come out with me. Normally I don't let anything interfere with my work but in your case I'm willing to make an exception."

She turned on him. "You take some beating for arrogance," she hissed furiously. "I wouldn't dream of interfering with your precious work so count me out and go back to your typewriter. You can work out your fantasies on that . . ."

"You have spirit – I like that," he broke in calmly, his eyes sweeping over her. "Mmm, very tempting, I must confess."

Bob stood up at that moment and indicated that he thought it was time to go. Since he had a very early rise each morning his wishes weren't unreasonable and as far as Katrina was concerned they were timely and welcome.

Getting to her feet she reached for her jacket but Larry Sinclair's anticipatory hands were there first, holding the garment as she shrugged herself into it, his hands sliding briefly over her arms before he drew away from her to lift his glass and down the remainder of his drink. "Hold on, I'll see you outside." He grabbed his jacket but didn't put it on as he strolled unhurriedly to the door. Several voices bade him goodnight and Katrina noticed they were mostly female.

It was a bitterly cold night. Stars studded the black reaches of the sky. The dark slopes of the Cairngorm mountains reared against the midnight blue of the horizon. The sweet, sharp air felt good to Katrina and she gulped it gratefully into her lungs.

Larry Sinclair was bidding goodnight to Belle and Bob. He didn't speak to Katrina and as he settled his long frame into a low, sleek sports car he seemed to have retreated into a world far removed from hers. He turned the ignition and a throaty roar from the engine split the peaceful night. He revved up and roared away and she watched his tail lights receding into the distance, feeling oddly bereft as the darkness swallowed him up.

"Come on, lass, it's freezing out here!" Belle's voice broke into her thoughts and though Bob told her to sit in the front with Belle she climbed into the back seat of the Morris, since all she wanted was to be quiet for a while and allow herself to unwind after the evening's experience.

She was glad to get back to the homely normality of Balgower Farm. The dogs barked from the shed where they spent their nights and a wanderlust cat came to wind itself round Belle's ankles as Bob turned the key in the door.

"I'll make the cocoa." Katrina went quickly to measure milk into a pan because she was aware that Belle was agog to know what had passed between her and Larry, and that was the last thing Katrina wished to discuss.

But Belle wasn't easily dissuaded. As they sat sipping steaming mugs of cocoa in front of the fire, she stroked the ears of a large marmalade tom on her knee and said boldly, "I know I asked you this before but I'm going to ask you again. What did you think of Larry Sinclair?"

Katrina shifted uncomfortably. "I thought I made that clear, Belle – anyway – I hardly know the man."

"You had plenty to say to each other just the same," persisted Belle, her lively eyes gleaming.

Katrina took a long draught of cocoa. "It was just small talk. You know how it is in a pub. There's always too much noise for people to be able to speak properly to one another." She had no intention of telling Belle that Larry had asked her to go out with him. She saw no point in saying anything since there was little likelihood that he would ask her again after she had been so adamant in her refusal.

She felt suddenly miserable. Why had she been so abrupt? Had it been something to do with the apprehension she felt every time thoughts of him wandered into her mind? Coupled with a blinding desire to be alone so that she could relive again those moments when his hands had touched her hair, her face. She shivered although the room was warm. He was dangerous – dangerous to be near. Belle had said he had a reputation for being a womaniser and she had no desire to repeat the experiences suffered at Paul's hands.

Bob rose and stretched. "Leave the lass alone, Belle," he chided. "She's only been here two minutes and already you're trying to involve her in things she obviously doesn't want to be mixed up in." He grinned and squeezed Katrina's shoulder affectionately. "She's a matchmaker is our Belle. Just you do what you want and don't listen to her. I'll say goodnight. Sleep well."

"I'll be up in a minute," Belle called after him as he retreated upstairs. She looked at Katrina and sighed. "Men! They don't know what they're talking about. You need to be taken out of yourself, Katrina, and Larry could do that very nicely. I know you had that unfortunate experience with Paul Carrington . . . your mother told me in a letter," she added at Katrina's look of enquiry. "He let you down badly but that doesn't mean all men are the same . . ."

"Oh, lord!" Katrina changed the subject quickly. "I forgot to phone Jilly."

The hands of the clock were at eleven and Belle shrugged her shoulders, "It isn't too late, surely? From what I gathered she's a young woman who keeps late hours."

"Mostly, but Jilly makes a point of having an early night on Sundays or she would never see the light of Monday morning." She shrugged and began to gather the mugs. "It doesn't matter, we didn't make any special arrangements. I'll ring her another time."

"Katrina," Belle caught her arm. "I'm not an interfering busybody. I just want you to be happy and to enjoy yourself. You're so young and haven't exactly been living it up lately. I want this to be a really special holiday – one that you'll remember." Her brown eyes were anxious and Katrina thought it was a great pity her father's cousin had never had children because she would have made a perfect mother. She compensated for the fact by always having young people around, but it wasn't quite the same.

Katrina smiled at her affectionately and hugged her.

"I know, and I don't think you're the least bit interfering, but you mustn't worry about me. I love being here and I'm going to make the most of every minute, so stop fussing." She linked her arm through the older woman's. "C'mon, let's go up. All this fresh air has tired me out and I want to get up early to see to those silly hens of yours. Honestly, I've never known creatures like them. It's something of an adventure to go collecting their eggs – a bit like a treasure trail that could lead anywhere."

Belle giggled. "Everything here is a bit unconventional I must admit, none of the animals stick to the rules; it's always been like that and I expect it always will be. It seems to work though, the hens are happy and happy hens mean lots of eggs. The cats and dogs nurse each other's babies and the spring lambs wander into the house whenever they see the door open. It's a sort of halfway-house for everybody but I don't mind; life is never dull and that's the way I like it."

They went upstairs in the best of spirits, but going to bed Katrina was annoyed to find herself still wide-awake. The bed was as warm and comfortable as last night, but even so she tossed and turned. Larry Sinclair invaded her thoughts and try how she would she couldn't exclude him.

The previous night she'd had her most refreshing sleep in weeks and she had imagined that would be the pattern of her stay at Balgower Farm. The peace of the countryside had soaked into her being and she'd planned long solitary walks in the glorious grandeur of Speyside. She had visualised contented days just mucking about on the farm; helping Belle in the kitchen, passing pleasant hours reading, poking about in the village shops for Christmas presents, or, if the weather was reasonable, riding through the crisp winter fields.

But all that had been before her meeting with Larry Sinclair and the unrest he created in her. Somehow he had spoiled it all, and she'd only just got here! Well, she wouldn't allow herself to become involved with him – not that he would want that anyway. He had asked her out certainly, but after her refusal he hadn't persisted any further; instead he had driven away in that flashy car of his without so much as a goodbye. Problem solved! Goodnight, Larry Sinclair!

She pulled the quilt about her shoulders and resolutely closed her eyes. An owl hooted from the birch wood; a dog barked from some distant farm. It was all so peaceful and she *had* to have peace to help her to get over the trauma of the last difficult weeks.

She imagined that she was sitting by her mother's bedside, reading her the Wordsworth poems that she had so loved. She heard her own voice inside her head: '*Sleep! by any stealth: So do not let me wear the night away: Without thee what is morning's wealth . . . ?*'

Chapter Five

"ARE you sure you won't come with me, Katrina?" Belle patted her hat into place and turned to look enquiringly at Katrina, seated at the table with a mug of tea in her hand. The kitchen was flooded with the searching rays of the December sun; the fragrance of bacon mingled with the subtle smell of dough which Belle had cut into rounds and placed on a tray ready to be popped into the oven.

Katrina nibbled a piece of toast and shook her head. "No, you go on, Belle. I've had enough of shops to last me for a while, though I will, of course, want to do some Christmas shopping. Not today, though, I'm quite content to stay here and look after things so that you can have some time to yourself. I'll put the scones in the oven." She smiled, her hazel eyes lighting. "Don't worry, I won't let them burn. I'm quite good at baking, actually. I did a fair amount of it while I was at home with Mum."

Belle studied her face. "You look a bit weary this morning, Katrina. Didn't you sleep well?"

"Not too badly," Katrina answered evasively. "I'll have a quiet morning pottering about. You go on now and don't worry about lunch, I'll have something prepared for you coming back."

"You're a good lass," Belle said warmly. "Jacky will be in with Bob at lunchtime, so set four places. There's a big pan of broth in the larder and plenty of ham to put into rolls and the scones will fill up any empty spaces that are left." She pulled on her gloves and went out to the shed where she kept her little green Mini. She had told Katrina to use the car whenever she wanted as she herself only used it occasionally to go shopping or to visit friends.

Katrina watched as Belle reversed out of the shed. The Mini had patches of red lead on the wings, similar to those on the Morris Traveller. One of the doors was tied with string and it was low on its axles. Katrina giggled as it hurtled unsteadily down the rutted road. Belle's driving reflected her nature: lively, energetic, and rather easygoing.

Left on her own for the first time since coming to Balgower, Katrina cleared the table before going into the porch to slip on a pair of wellingtons and an anorak.

Stepping outside, she filled her lungs with sweet hill air. It was a glorious day. The sky was a deep azure blue stretching away to embrace the peaks of the hills. Because Balgower Farm was snuggled well back into a spruce-covered slope it afforded a panoramic view of the Spey Valley. Tawny tracts of moor merged into green fields studded with lochans. Rivers sparkled in the sun, flanked by rowans and silver birches.

The glistening white hills of the Cairngorms looked sleek and low against the sky but Katrina knew that their height was deceptive from this distance. She had seen them close at hand and knew that the peaks were rugged and awe-inspiring and at least one of the ski runs rose to a height of over four thousand feet.

The sharp, clean air caressed her face and in minutes her cheeks were glowing. She scattered feed for the hens and collected the eggs that had been deposited in various nesting places. Belle's hens were as carefree as their mistress, and Katrina chuckled when she found two eggs laid neatly in the rim of an old car tyre.

Absently, she put them into her basket. She could have spent this holiday in complete contentment – if only Larry Sinclair hadn't come into her life. Since meeting him she had felt restless and nervy and full of strange, anticipatory apprehension.

She sighed and pushed her hair back from her face. It was ridiculous. She had only spoken to him briefly – yet the very memory of him flooded her being with warmth. He filled her thoughts constantly and she had had to exert a great deal of willpower coming downstairs that morning to behave normally and pretend that everything in her life was as it had been on her arrival at Balgower Farm. She wanted only solitude in order to be alone with her thoughts and to her shame she had been relieved when Belle had announced her intention of going off to do some shopping in Aviemore village.

Bob had gone off before Katrina came down, but she had looked from her window to see him driving away on a tractor piled high with winter feed for the ewes wintering on the foothills.

She stood for some minutes, gazing dreamily over the landscape, before going back into the kitchen to put the eggs in the pantry. Popping the tray of scones into the oven she put the kettle on to boil for coffee and went to the sink to wash her hands. Lifting her head she glimpsed herself in the mirror. Her hair was mussed and a streak of dirt lay over one cheek. Musingly, she decided she looked healthier than two days ago when she set off from London. Two days! They had flown yet somehow had stood still. Not a great deal had happened, yet she felt something momentous had changed in her life.

London seemed to belong to another age. Everything that meant anything was here in Speyside. Startled by such strange ideas, she quickly dried her hands and went to rescue the kettle which was whistling loudly on the hotplate. But before she could go and search out the coffee jar the cats decided they wanted to be fed and wound themselves so persistently round her legs she was obliged to set some saucers on the floor and fill them with milk.

Then there came the sound of a vehicle stopping outside, the next minute the door opened and the postman popped his head round. "Mornin', Miss," he said with a cheery nod. "Belle not in today?" He had come further into the room as he spoke, his eyes gently panning first the table and then the little hotplate on the stove where Belle usually kept the teapot simmering. It didn't seem to matter if it was stewed, Bob drank it avidly, so too did his wife, both of them sipping away happily at the steaming mugfuls as if they were tasting nectar.

"I rinsed out the pot," Katrina explained to the newcomer. "But if you like, I'll make some more, unless of course, you'd rather have coffee? The kettle's on the boil."

"Na," he shook his head decidedly, "it's tea for me, lass. The first and last time I drank coffee it gave me heartburn so I've stuck to the good old brew ever since."

"Even the stewed variety?" Katrina asked with a smile.

"Especially that, it's the only sort they make round here," he told her with a grin. "By the way, I'm Joe the Post, and I've heard all about you from Belle and Bob. I mind your folks well, me and your father had many a fine talk together and your mother was a bonny woman. She used to make these funny wee things she called horse's dovers, but they tasted good anyway despite their name, though I always did wonder what she put in them."

Katrina gave a shout of laughter and, holding out her hand, she shook his warmly. "Pleased to meet you, Joe, you deserve a cup of tea after all that and you've chosen the right moment to arrive." She withdrew the scones from the oven, piping hot and beautifully risen.

"Well, well, now, like mother like daughter. They look good enough to eat and'll go down a treat with a nice cup of hot tea."

They sat in the kitchen, companionably eating scones and drinking tea until Joe decided regretfully that he had better get on with his rounds. Between them they had eaten their way through a fair number of scones; Katrina surprising herself with an appetite that seemed to have grown and grown since coming to Balgower.

Belle would come back expecting to have enough home baking to fill the men at lunchtime and with this in mind Katrina decided to make another batch, soon wielding the rolling pin with such energy she sent clouds of flour into the air.

The crunch of wheels on gravel made her jerk up her head. Surely not Belle back already! And this mess waiting for her! Hurriedly, she wiped her floury hands on a tea-towel and made to go over to the window. But before she had taken two steps the door opened and Larry Sinclair walked in, moving with that slow, easy grace she remembered so well.

Katrina's hand flew up to brush away her hair from her warm face. She had enveloped herself in one of Belle's white cotton aprons and she was aghast to think he had arrived to find her in a complete mess.

He came further into the room and said teasingly, "Well, well, what have we here? A real domestic little scene and no mistake."

"What – what are you doing here?" She hated herself for stammering. He was filling the room with his presence and the sight of him sent a strange shiver trembling through her body.

"I was hoping to catch you on your own," he said, with disarming frankness.

With a great effort she pulled herself together. "Belle isn't here. She's gone shopping." Katrina was relieved that her voice came out cool and even.

"I know, she always does on a Monday," he drawled lazily. She took a step backwards, her hands fumbling with the apron fastenings. "Here, let me help you." With a few long strides he covered the distance which separated them and expertly dispensed with the knotted tapes that held the apron in place. The unflattering layers of cotton fell away from her slender figure and his blue gaze swept appreciatively over her. She noticed that his mouth was wide and sensuous, uplifted at one corner in an expression of wry amusement. But the intent look in his eyes as they fastened on her mouth belied his smile and she pulled in her breath and turned quickly away.

"Belle will be back soon." She had put more emphasis than intended into the words and hoped fervently that she hadn't given the impression of being afraid to be alone in the house with him.

But she was afraid! Afraid of what his presence was doing to her. She felt stifled; her heart was behaving strangely, her legs felt like pieces of jelly and she knew it wasn't him she was afraid of, it was of herself, of her inability to behave normally in his company.

She couldn't deny, even if she wanted to, that he was the most disturbing man she had ever met. Frantically, she tried to remember her reaction to Paul on their first meeting. She had been pleased, flattered, taken aback, but all these things put together were nothing to what she felt now. Larry Sinclair had barely touched her, yet she was devastated by him. The very sight of him invoked in her a yearning that was beyond her experience. She couldn't handle it . . . and she wasn't even going to try. She had to make it plain that she wanted nothing to do with him.

"Shouldn't you put those in the oven?" The cool notes of his voice penetrated her senses like drops of freezing rain.

"Oh yes, of course," she lifted the trays of scones and carried them over to the stove, glad that a few feet of breathing space now existed between herself and Larry Sinclair. She spent longer than necessary arranging the trays inside the oven then stood up, and without turning, said, "Would you like a cup of coffee? Or tea? I've just had some with the postman, but I don't mind making more of either." Without waiting for his reply she rattled cups onto saucers and for the second time that morning, set down the sugar bowl and cream jug on the table.

"The postman, eh? In other circumstances I might be jealous, but I take it you mean Joe, middle-aged, married for donkeys years, more interested in shinty than in anything else, so I'll let it pass this once."

"Bully for you!" she returned scathingly. "And you haven't told me what you want. Coffee or tea?"

"I want you."

The words fell with calculated deliberation and if it was reaction he was seeking, he certainly got it. Katrina felt a tremor go through her and she lowered the kettle back onto the hotplate. Her heart had accelerated madly. Taking a deep breath she swung round to face him and said coldly, "I beg your pardon, Mr Sinclair."

"Aw, c'mon, drop the formalities. I'm Larry to my friends, and I hope I can count you as one of those." He stood in the middle of the room, his thumbs hooked into the belt loops of his close-fitting trousers. She couldn't help noticing how long his legs were and she tore her eyes away to look him straight in the eye. He was wearing an Aran sweater; it was a bulky, heavy knit but even so his broad chest strained against it and his face looked very tanned in contrast to the creamy wool.

"*Mr* Sinclair," she repeated firmly. "Last night you led me to believe you were something of a recluse – that your writing took precedence over all else – so, just what *are* you doing here?"

He ran his fingers through sun-bleached hair and regarded her steadily. "Call it an inability to concentrate.

When the face of a beautiful girl haunts you on every blank page, the muse doesn't stand an earthly. As I told you, I know Belle goes out on a Monday morning so I came over hoping to find you here alone. I had an idea you might not have gone with her – after all, you can get to shops anytime in London so, putting myself in your place, I figured you might stay behind – and it turns out I was right."

The look in his hooded blue eyes made her catch her breath. Somehow she felt he knew exactly what was going on in her mind; that he knew how much he disturbed her, and that no matter how calm she might outwardly appear he knew that inwardly she was finding great difficulty in controlling her emotions.

She took a deep breath and spread her hands in appeal, "Look, I'm busy. I promised Belle to have lunch ready. Also, there's this mess to clear up—"

"Wasn't there some mention of coffee?" he interrupted smoothly. He shook his head and sighed. "I can see you aren't used to country ways. Haven't you ever heard of Highland hospitality? It's supposed to take precedence over everything . . ."

"I am *not* a country person and I am *not* Highland."

"Really? With a name like Cameron? And all these years here was I believing that your father came from these parts . . ."

Her face flamed. "He did."

"And that makes you—?"

Pride in her Scottish blood made her cry out defensively, "All right! Yes! I am of Highland stock but you're just splitting hairs! What I am and where I come from has nothing at all to do with the fact that you seem to have come here with the sole intention of ridiculing me."

"That's a bit strong." His irritation showed in the tightening of his jaw. "I only came here to be friendly. Where's the harm in that?"

"Oh – none. It's just – you have rather a strange way of saying things."

"I don't mean it." His sudden smile had a softening effect. "Let's make up over a cup of tea – I prefer it to coffee."

She smiled back. "Like Joe, Dad too, he always preferred it to anything else and said it was Scotland's national drink – after whisky. All right. Sit down, I'm sorry, I should have invited you sooner. I have a lot to learn about Highland hospitality." He sat down, gazing at her. "I'll just warm the pot," she said, and felt foolish when she dropped a spoon on the floor in her haste to be doing something positive.

"Butter fingers," he chided gently and, bending to pick up the spoon, he placed it on the table, leaned back, folded his arms, and waited.

Chapter Six

THE tea caddy was empty. Very conscious of his eyes watching her she crossed the floor and went into the pantry to reach up to the shelf where Belle kept her stores. Clutching at a packet of tea she froze suddenly and the hairs on her neck rose. Turning very slowly she saw that her way was blocked. Larry Sinclair was standing in the doorway, one hand braced against the door jamb, the thumb of the other hooked once more into the belt loop of his trousers. His tall frame filled the small space, the top of his head only just clearing the beam. One long leg was crossed casually over the other, his lips lifted into a careless little smile, his eyes alert and intense.

She straightened her shoulders and ignoring her fast-beating heart she said firmly, "Will you get out of my way, please?"

"No." The refusal jumped out at her. "Why should I?"

"Because I-I want you to."

"Do you? Can you stand there and look me straight in the eye and convince me that that's what you really want?"

"Oh, please, stop this – this nonsense. I really don't want to argue with you but—"

"Who's arguing?" he said reasonably. "I just want to admire that's all. Surely it's no great offence to appreciate beauty?" His eyes travelled over her legs, lingered for some moments on her breasts, before coming to rest on her face. "Something happened between us last night," his voice was soft, "you know it and I know it and if you try to deny it, you would be lying."

"For heaven's sake!" she banged the packet of tea back on the shelf and faced him with clenched fists. "I'm not going to admit or deny anything. I just want you to let me out of here – *please*," she appealed. "I have things to do."

"So have I." His hand slid down the door jamb and that very action made her retreat backwards a step. "Are you afraid of me?" he asked abruptly.

"Don't be ridiculous!" Her mouth had gone dry. "Who do you think you are? Oh, I suppose some women might fawn over you and no doubt you're used to being idolised by people in general but I don't come into that category! To me you're just another man – that's all."

His smile widened. "I see. You sound as though you've chalked up dozens of them yet your behaviour suggests otherwise, and while I may be all sorts of swine I wouldn't like to be accused of the attempted seduction of a complete innocent."

"You arrogant beast!" she fumed and quite unintentionally added, "If it's any of your business there *was* someone . . ."

"Was?"

"Yes – was – but like you he proved to be a conceited womaniser."

"Oh, come on, one minute you want me to think you

know nothing about me and in the next breath you accuse me of philandering."

"Oh, I didn't mean that, forget it." She had difficulty getting the words to come out evenly. She was intensely aware of him, of his strong brown hands, his virility. She tried to tear her eyes away from him but was powerless to do so. She noticed the fair hairs on the back of his hands, saw the muscles in his legs tightening as he uncrossed them and began to walk towards her. She was caught in a trance, unable to move away or control what was happening to her. Without a word he raised his hand and ran his forefinger over her jawline. "No – please, you mustn't do that," she gasped, turning her head away from him, but there was no escaping his probing fingers. She moved back a step but the shelves of the pantry effectively forestalled her.

"I must," he murmured quietly and his mouth came down firmly on hers.

His lips were cool on contact but almost immediately became warm. Over and over he kissed her but in a way that was tender and undemanding and she was aware that relief was chasing the tension from her body. She had imagined roughness, the way it had been with Paul. Larry was so strong, yet his touch on her mouth was like thistledown, and she felt her limbs loosening. Why shouldn't she enjoy what was happening to her? It seemed so right, so natural, to let Larry kiss her. After all, she wouldn't be in Scotland long enough for anything to come of it, so why deny herself these moments in his arms?

Then everything began to change, the pressure of his mouth was more insistent now and she had no will to deny him. Instead she allowed herself to respond to him and a shaft of warmth spread through her as she sensed his urgency. His hand came up to cradle her head and she melted further against him. Minutes passed in which he played with her mouth and the relaxation in her reverted to an eagerness for something more. His arms enclosed her body, she knew a need to touch him, to caress him as he was caressing her, and with a soft little moan of resignation she raised her hands to grasp the firm flesh of his shoulders.

His tongue probed her mouth, he groaned and crushed her against him, one hand moving over the small of her back to her hips, the fingers of the other tracing the curve of her ear before moving to the top of her spine. Her body became ever more pliant. Willingly she moulded herself against him, the last of her resistance melting away in a great surging wave of desire, when his mouth moved to her ears to nuzzle them.

Wonderful sensations trembled through her and, closing her eyes, she responded to him with an urgency she had never known before. She could feel his heart throbbing against her breasts but as she opened her eyes and glimpsed the hard, intense lines of his face, an unease niggled through her. The skin of his neck was damp with perspiration, a memory of Paul pierced her mind and her unease intensified as she recalled his rage when she wouldn't submit to him . . .

But this wasn't Paul, this was Larry, awakening her body to pleasures beyond all dreams, allaying her fears, carrying her with him on waves of excitement, invoking in her a sweet, raw craving that robbed her of every shred of willpower she possessed. His lips, his hands, his body, promising delights beyond compare . . .

"Someone's coming." His voice, hoarse with longing, invaded her senses and she had to force herself back to reality. Dazedly she stared at him, noting the flush high on his cheekbones.

"What – what did you say?"

"Someone's coming – Belle, I think."

As she struggled to compose herself she was aware of the kitchen door opening. The sound seemed to come from a long way off yet drove into her with the force of a sledgehammer. As she came back to normality other impressions jetted in on her, one upon the other. The smell of burning assailed her nostrils, she uttered a cry of consternation as she rushed to the oven and almost burned her fingers. Shakily she reached for the oven glove and opened the door to stare disbelievingly inside.

"Damn and blast!" she groaned as she withdrew a tray of charred remnants and rattled it onto the table. "Please don't let this be happening to me!"

"Looks as if it already has."

She spun round to find Belle watching her with some bemusement and burst out, "Oh, Belle, I'm sorry. I-I forgot all about them," she finished rather lamely.

"Och, don't worry, I've done it often enough myself." There was a twinkle in Belle's eyes which made Katrina wonder if she had guessed the reason behind her carelessness. Of course, she knows! Katrina told herself. Belle's no fool. Larry's car is outside for everyone to see.

"Aren't you early?" she asked, mentally wondering just how much time she and Larry had spent locked in each other's arms.

Belle pulled off her hat and threw it onto a chair. "A bit late as a matter of fact. It's almost lunchtime."

"Is it? Oh, lord! I promised to have it ready and look at this mess!" Katrina's legs still felt shaky and she had to force herself to fetch a cloth and start wiping the flour from the table.

"Good morning, Belle." Larry's casual greeting brought some normality back into the situation, for which Katrina was heartily grateful.

"I thought it was you I saw in the pantry," Belle said mildly.

"We were going to have a cup of tea." Katrina sounded too matter-of-fact and her pink cheeks showed that she knew it.

"I see you didn't quite make it." Belle eyed the tea things on the table and her mouth quirked into a smile.

"My fault, Belle, all of it." Larry sounded infuriatingly calm.

"I haven't a doubt of that," Belle nodded. "I imagine you arrived on Katrina just as she was in the middle of baking, and of course in her rush to make tea for you, everything got burnt."

"That's it, exactly."

They sounded like a couple of conspirators and if Katrina hadn't thought it too ridiculous for words she might have thought they'd set the whole thing up. She went to get the pan of soup from the pantry and returned in time to hear Belle asking Larry to stay to lunch, but he declined and as he moved over to the door Katrina hardly dared look at him. A quick glance however showed that he wasn't quite as composed as he was making out. A

58

muscle in his jaw betrayed his inner feelings and somehow this tugged at her heart, even though a warning voice beat deep inside her head.

She had vowed she wouldn't become emotionally serious with a man again and knew that if she ever allowed herself to be alone once more with Larry, she couldn't trust herself to keep those vows.

"How would you like to have dinner with me?" She met his eyes and saw that they were laden with intimacy. The memory of his mouth pressed against hers was so strong it was as if she was lying once more in his embrace.

At his question she fought a fierce inner battle with herself. What he suggested sounded safe enough. As long as she wasn't alone with him it would be all right . . . But her better senses warned her against it. She couldn't risk being hurt again and a mild relationship with Larry Sinclair didn't seem possible. Just to look at him made her reel with desire to be kissed by him beyond resistance. "I'm sorry – but no. I never did eat a big dinner, and you know what some restaurants are like . . ."

"Lunch then?" he persisted. Again she met his keen gaze and felt her resolve weakening. She had to be strong, she had to. Stiffly she shook her head and saw his mouth tightening. "I take it you *do* eat?" His tones dripped sarcasm. "Could you manage a snack? Or is it not so much *what* you eat but *who* you eat with?"

She opened her mouth to make a sharp retort but at this point Belle intervened. "Oh, go on, Katrina," she didn't look up as she set cutlery on the table. "It will do you the world of good to get out of the house. You're only young once. Take my advice and enjoy it."

Katrina realised she was trapped. To refuse Larry's invitation would seem childish and in the last two minutes he had already succeeded in making her arguments seem trite. "Okay," she conceded lamely.

"Good," his voice held a note of triumph. "I'll pick you up around midday tomorrow. Wear something warm." He smiled at her easily before hoisting himself away from the doorpost to go out. She watched as he walked over to the red MG and folded himself lithely in behind the steering wheel. The engine fired and with a roar he was off, his hand appearing briefly from the window in an indolent wave.

The swift arrival of Bob and Jacky interrupted her thoughts and she immersed herself in helping to serve lunch. As they all sat round the table chatting she was glad that Larry receded into the back of her mind. Jacky's lively description of his morning's work with the sheep made her laugh and as the talk switched to his forthcoming marriage and the financial difficulties of setting up a home, she entered into the discussions with zest, even managing to put forth some practical hints on thrifty housekeeping.

That afternoon she went with Belle to visit an aged relative whom she knew vaguely as Aunt Annie, though she wasn't an aunt at all but had ties with the Cameron family through marriage. Aunt Annie lived in a croft beside Loch Insh. She was dour and gruff with wispy, snow white hair and a generous nose and she was wearing a long black dress, a baggy green cardigan, and a white apron that reached to her feet.

Setting foot inside her crofthouse was like stepping

back fifty years. A sense of timelessness lay everywhere: photographs and old china abounded, an ancient organ sat in a corner of the living room, its surface covered by lace doilies on which stood more pictures and little silver trophies won in gymkhanas from a bygone age.

Katrina was fascinated by all she saw and even more by Aunt Annie herself who, hard though she seemed to be, had a soft spot for the scrawny tortoiseshell cats who came to wind themselves round her black-clad legs and mew up into her face as she drank tea and ate the cakes that Belle had brought.

"I still bake myself, you know," she barked to no one in particular. "People think you can't do anything when you get to my age but that's where they're wrong, I can still look after myself and I'll never go to one of those homes they have for old people."

"They wouldn't take an old tearaway like you," Belle chuckled, "but if you want to stay here on your own you'll have to keep fit, so how would you like it if we wrapped you up and took you for a walk by the loch?"

Aunt Annie gave a horse-like snort. "I hate these tame walks people insist on taking me on. There's nothing to read. Far better a cemetery where you can see people's life stories on the stones and get the fresh air into the bargain. Besides, I'd like fine to go and visit Jeemie, it's a long time since I said hello to him."

"All right, if that's what you want," Belle agreed, and they piled into the Mini to drive to the graveyard where Aunt Annie's husband, Jeemie, was buried. It was a peaceful place, set on a pine-clad hillock with views of the surrounding countryside. Even so, Katrina shivered a little as she glanced around at the moss-covered headstones, memories of her mother's funeral still vivid in her mind.

As it happened, Aunt Annie was enough to make anybody forget anything. She was sublimely happy browsing around, pausing for a few moments of quiet at Jeemie's grave, moving on to others and asking Katrina to read out the inscriptions on the stones. "I'll soon be pushing up the daisies myself, you know," she cackled wickedly. "Though mind, I've a few things to see to first and won't go before I'm ready."

She looked at Katrina and an understanding expression came into her eyes. "Don't be sad, lassie, I know all about your mother and how you nursed her. It's hard to take, I know, but think of it this way. She and your father are together again, the waiting is done with. I've been lonely all these years without my Jeemie; the only person in the world who really understood me. For each of us there's someone, and when they go things are never the same again. If you can think of your parents that way it will be easier for you and you can get on with living your own life."

"Thank you, Aunt Annie." Katrina reached out and hugged the old lady, then led her down to the Mini where Belle was enjoying forty winks, having had enough of cemeteries for one day.

When Katrina rang Peggy Melville that evening she was tempted to mention Larry, but decided against it. Peggy was delighted to hear from her.

"I got your letter saying you were coming north for a holiday," her calm, sweet voice came soothingly over the line. "I was so sorry about your mother, Katie, a break will do you the world of good."

"I'll come to see you as soon as I can, Peggy," Katrina smiled as her friend voiced her delight. She had last seen Peggy when she was a bridesmaid at her wedding and she had almost forgotten the calming effect her friend had had in her life.

Before her marriage Peggy had worked in a dress shop a few blocks away from the MoD offices and, with Jilly, they had often made a threesome for lunch, though Katrina had often got the impression that Peggy only tolerated Jilly for the sake of keeping the peace.

Despite her even temperament Peggy was extremely perceptive, and she had said to Katrina on more than one occasion that she knew Jilly was inclined to criticise her behind her back; a fact which Katrina had neither confirmed nor refuted as she knew only too well the truth of Peggy's words.

Goodbyes were said, she put the phone down and dialled Jilly's number, determined that she would give no hint that anything out of the ordinary had happened to her. Jilly asked if she was bored and she said vehemently, "Good heavens no! Anything but."

"Hmm,"Jilly sounded thoughtful. "I believe you mean it. You sound sort of keyed up."

Katrina forced a laugh. "Really, you're imagining things."

"No I'm not," Jilly said with conviction. "You sound as if something exciting has happened to you and you're trying your damndest to hide it."

Katrina experienced a pang of resentment. Jilly had a knack of ferreting out secrets and often she managed to get Katrina to disclose things she wanted to keep to herself. Katrina had never really minded but on this occasion she was more guarded and briskly changed the subject, for once turning the tables by asking Jilly a stream of questions about her own affairs and thus diverting attention away from hers. There followed a lively exchange of small talk before a rather breathless Jilly decided she had better say goodnight.

Katrina returned the phone to its cradle, finding an odd satisfaction in having kept her innermost thoughts to herself. To have had Jilly asking questions about a man she knew little enough of herself would have seemed like an invasion of her privacy. She had no desire just now to share Larry Sinclair with Jilly or anyone else for that matter.

Chapter Seven

KATRINA lifted her jacket from the bed and, throwing it over her arm, she ran downstairs to stand rather self-consciously in the kitchen doorway. The others were at lunch but when she appeared Jacky raised his red head to look at her and let out an appreciative whistle. Bob poked him with his elbow. "You'll embarrass the lass," he chided.

"It's okay, Bob," Katrina said with a smile in Jacky's direction, "I'm getting used to him now."

Bob picked up his soup spoon to get on with the business of eating but Belle twisted in her chair, her brown eyes absorbing with approval the sight of Katrina clad in a green trouser suit. The colour enhanced her shining strands of chestnut hair and the flecks of green in her eyes. "You know what sort of things suit you, Katrina," Belle said approvingly. "You look a real treat."

"Ay, lass, you do that," Bob agreed.

To escape the open admiration in Jacky's eyes Katrina bent to adjust the zip of her boots just as the powerful and unmistakable roar of Larry Sinclair's car thundered into the kitchen.

Katrina fought down a rising sense of apprehension. She had anticipated yet dreaded this moment. Since yesterday she had felt herself to be teetering on the edge of a cliff, knowing that to put one foot forward was to risk plunging into the unknown. To remain safe all she had to do was step backwards, but she knew it was already too late for that.

She could never go back now, she *had* to go forward, but she would do so with the utmost caution. Three times since yesterday she had gone to the phone with the intention of putting Larry off, but each time she had been prevented by the thought that to do so might seem to him an admission of weakness. She would have to go through with seeing him, but she would behave very coolly. She must have appeared rather naïve to him with all her stammering and blushing, but from now on it would be different.

Her vows lasted the short time it took to walk out to his car. The sight of his tall, arresting figure immediately destroyed any defences she had built up. He was wearing a duffel jacket with the collar pushed up against the brown skin of his neck, as although it was another blue sunny day it was bitterly cold with an east wind blowing. His sun-bleached hair was more startling than ever against the blue vault of the sky, and Katrina experienced a strong urge to reach up and run her fingers through it.

His eyes flicked over her. "Perfect," he approved, taking her hand to help her into the car. His palm was cool in hers and as he walked round and slid in behind the wheel she couldn't trust herself to say anything so she remained silent till they got to the bottom of the farm track.

As they turned onto the main road, Katrina endeavoured to make conversation, though she was very aware that the confines of the car forced them into an uncomfortable intimacy with his hand brushing her knee every time he changed gear. "Where are we going?"

He pressed his foot down on the accelerator and made a smooth change from top to third as they slowed down behind a tractor. "Wait and see," he answered briefly.

After that Katrina made no more attempts to converse as it was difficult to be heard above the sound of the engine. She settled back and watched the countryside flashing past. The MG was smooth and comfortable and easily ate up the miles. Her initial nerves began to give way to a joyous excitement as they sped past the pine forests of Rothiemurchus and made for Loch Morlich. Here, despite the cold, there were several parties of people enjoying picnics on the white sandy shores that bordered the loch.

In no time at all they were on a wide, steep mountain road on which driving conditions were good despite the fact that the slopes on either side were snow-covered. "We're on Coire Cas," Katrina observed, gazing round her happily. "I was ten years old last time I was here. Dad brought us out for the day and I've never forgotten it."

"It's all changed a bit since then," Larry said as he drove into the car park high up in the Cairngorm mountains. He switched off the engine and grinned at her. "Now you know why I asked you to put on warm clothing. I thought this would make a change from the usual. You have a choice. You can have a snack lunch at the White Lady Sheiling or we can take the chairlift to the Ptarmigan Observation Restaurant."

"Oh, let's take the chairlift to the top!" Katrina cried.

His smile deepened. "I was hoping you would say that. I'll go and get the tickets." He got out of the car to make his way to the Sheiling where the tickets were sold for the ski lifts.

Katrina looked at the sparkling white slopes dotted with colourful skiers and a deep joy filled her being. It was all so different from other first dates and trust Larry to pick on something that appealed to her sense of adventure. She had always loved outdoor pursuits and had often wondered if she would have been happier living in the country. She watched him coming back to the car, his measured stride carrying him easily over the snowy ground, and she could just imagine him gliding along on skis – on a surfboard too for that matter, or on the back of a horse. He was the sort of man who would fit easily into the outdoor scene, yet for all she knew he might not enjoy any of these things and could just as well be a night owl who revelled in parties and nightclubs. Then she remembered he'd mentioned skiing two nights ago in the inn at Nethy, so that was perhaps one thing they might have in common anyway.

He held open the door of the MG and she climbed out to stare enchanted at the scene far below. Loch Morlich was a deep blue puddle surrounded by the glens and hills of Speyside. It was an amazing vista, one that made her catch her breath and feel small and rather insignificant.

"Put this on." He was holding out her jacket and she slipped her arms into it. He swung her round to face him and as he reached forward she thought for a moment he was going to kiss her.

Instead, he pulled her hood up and for a few seconds

he held her captive. His mouth was very close to hers and suddenly she had difficulty in breathing. Not wishing to appear disturbed in any way she forced herself to stay quite still, her head slightly tilted back.

She was a picture with the fur trim of her hood framing her face. One or two tendrils of hair had escaped and, taking one, he wound it round his fingers before letting her go. "C'mon." Taking her hand he led her towards the chairlift. They climbed into one of the chairs, and her stomach lurched as the lift began to operate. Larry's arm came round the back of the seat to rest lightly on her shoulders; his touch was somehow very comforting. "You've been in Switzerland – you must have done this before?"

"Oh yes, I have," she didn't look at him, "but it was quite a long time ago. Don't worry, it won't take me long to get used to it again. It's an experience, being up here, seeing the ground gliding away, feeling the cold air rushing past."

As they rose higher she forgot her nerves. The sun was dazzling in the sky, the corries of the frosted white ridges were filled with shadows, the steel towers of the lift marched up the slopes in front; the reds and blues of the skiers were like jewels scattered in the snow.

By the time they reached the Ptarmigan Restaurant, Katrina discovered she was ravenous. She had eaten little at breakfast and the sharp mountain air combined with the savoury smells inside the dome-shaped building put an edge on her appetite.

They chose a table near a window which afforded breathtaking views of Strathspey. It was like sitting on top of the world and even if it was just for a little while, Katrina knew it was a memory that would remain with her for always.

They each had a bowl of thick, warming soup followed by chicken legs and French fries, and she enjoyed it all thoroughly, though all the time she was eating she was very conscious of Larry's nearness.

"I would like to buy you a proper meal sometime," he said, his voice serious.

"That was a proper meal," she answered lightly. "The sort I like: informal and relaxed."

With scant regard for etiquette he put his elbows on the table and studied her face. She noticed that his nails were chewed and when he saw her looking he held out his hands to study them. "They'll grow – my nails, I mean – when I finish the book." His mouth twisted into a rueful grin.

"I wasn't being critical."

"No, well I am." The pupils of his eyes grew dark. "I am looking at your face very critically – especially the freckles on your nose."

She was immediately alert. "Oh? Do I still have them? They usually fade in the winter."

"Yes, they're still there, of all the things I remember about you, your freckles are the most outstanding feature." She coloured a little, wondering if he was going to insult her. He continued to speak, his eyes watching her. "The sun used to make them more pronounced and you hated it when I teased you and called you a freckled witch." He remembered as much as that? She grew more uncomfortable and looked away. "No, don't do that," his voice was soft. "You have grown from a ponytailed kid into a rather lovely young woman. I'm glad you kept your freckles though."

She had never liked the sprinkling of freckles on the bridge of her nose and had tried everything to get rid of them; therefore it came as something of a pleasant surprise to know he regarded them as a beauty asset. He took one of her hands and stroked it, his thumb lingering on her palm. "Tell me about yourself, Katie."

"There's nothing to tell. You seem to know all about me."

"Surface things only. What about your likes and dislikes? The type of man you go for? This boyfriend of yours, for instance – the one you mentioned yesterday – what's he like?"

"Paul Carrington isn't mine, not now – nor ever was for that matter . . . He was ambitious – he wanted to get on in life and he didn't seem to want to do it with me. I was looking after my mother and couldn't spare enough time for him . . ." she halted, unwilling to let Paul spoil her enjoyment of the afternoon. In the last few days she had barely given him a thought. The very mention of his name was an intrusion into the scene.

"In other words, he was a bit of a bastard," Larry stated firmly, and to her surprise she saw that he meant what he said.

"It's over now," she said dismissively. "I don't want to talk about it."

"Paul Carrington," he said thoughtfully. "The name rings a vague kind of bell." He shrugged, "I might have met him sometime – or maybe he's just like a lot of other chaps I've come across."

"The world is full of them."

71

She couldn't keep a note of bitterness out of her voice, but if she'd wanted reaction she was disappointed. He merely turned down the corners of his mouth and drawled, "Men like me, for instance?"

She raised her brows. "If the glove fits . . ." Then, feeling that she sounded rather too harsh, she added, "You might be, I suppose."

"You suppose nothing, somebody put the idea in your head – unless of course you think you know more about me than you make out."

"Sorry to disappoint you but I don't. In all innocence Belle happened to mention that there was some gossip concerning your affairs with women. Belle was on your side, I might add."

"Good for Belle." His eyes held a hint of mockery. "In my own defence I can only say that, when I'm writing a book, I leave 'em all wondering where I'm hiding myself. Only kidding, of course, by now they have a pretty good idea that I come north to work, yet none of them seem to love me enough to come trailing up here looking for me. I don't see a queue, do you?" Katrina said nothing and his lips twisted into a devilish grin. "At the moment you're my only admirer. I've extended the rules and decided to make you an exception."

Katrina felt her colour deepening. "You flatter yourself, don't you?"

He grinned unrepentantly, "Since I don't have my supposed female entourage to feed my vanity – yes, I suppose I do, it keeps the adrenalin flowing."

Feeling herself on shaky ground, Katrina changed the subject. She was conscious that a few curious looks were being cast in Larry's direction and it made her aware that, as well as being the most exciting man she had ever met, he was also something of a well-known personality. Till then she had been so taken up by his magnetism she had almost forgotten about his work. She cupped her chin in her hands and regarded him quizzically. Not wanting to sound over-impressed by his achievements she said in a matter-of-fact voice, "Belle tells me you sometimes appear on television – to talk about your books."

"You know, you've got wonderful eyes." He was deliberately keeping the conversation on a personal level and she straightened up, her tone a shade more chilly as she said, "For goodness sake, can't you ever be serious?"

"Very, when the occasion demands it," he assured her with maddening calm. "At the moment I don't want to talk about me – I want to know more about you. I find myself at a disadvantage with you. Though you are unflatteringly ignorant about my affairs, you still seem to know enough about them to give you the edge over me. Belle has told me some things about you but there's still some filling in to be done. To be honest I'm flummoxed. The last time we met I was about sixteen and you must have been ten. In other words you were a flat-chested, unsophisticated little kid – *now* . . ." His narrowed eyes flicked over her in a slow assessment and she felt herself growing rigid with embarrassment.

"Stop that!" she hissed.

His eyes widened in surprise. "Stop what? I find you a very fascinating young woman. From a skinny, awkward little girl you have blossomed into a distinctly desirable creature. Paul What's-his-name must have been mad to let you go."

She wasn't certain if he was joking or not, yet she couldn't help feeling flattered by his words. Being with him was like going up and down in a lift; one minute he was saying things that made her wary of him, the next she was feeling so good she could have laughed aloud with happiness. Leaning towards him she said lightly, "I can see why you became a writer. I have no doubt you say such poetic things to – to . . ." she floundered, and to hide her confusion she seized her paper napkin and began to fold it neatly.

"To all women," he finished smoothly. "No, not quite. Those that have passed my way were unknown to me as children. You and I share the unique experience of having crossed paths before. Don't you find it a rather intriguing situation?"

His bold stare compelled her to answer. "It's not all that unusual, surely, a lot of people must have had the same experience?"

"I disagree. Taken as a whole it's perhaps ordinary enough, but in our case I think it was meant. A second chance to get to know one another."

The words were laden with too many meanings and she didn't know how to deal with them. She'd vowed to herself that she wouldn't see him again, yet she could have sat listening to his slow, deep voice for hours. A glance at her watch showed her that the afternoon had flown, but she was no nearer to finding out more about him than she'd been when they started off.

He had noticed her action and begun to uncurl his long legs. "You're letting me know we ought to be going . . ." He glanced at her empty plates. "Not bad for someone on a starvation diet."

74

"I'm not on any sort of diet."

"You could have fooled me."

"What do you mean?"

"At a guess I'd say this Paul character gave you such a bad time you went on a sort of self-imposed hunger strike against men in general . . ."

She stared at him incredulously, her face red with humiliation. "That's pure conjecture. A load of-of imaginative rubbish not worthy of any writer of whatever status!"

"Is it?" The line of his jaw had tensed. "Not to put too fine an edge on it, I'd guess you've denied yourself any male company for too long. You give the impression of holding back – as if you're afraid—"

"That's ridiculous and impertinent," she said hotly. "I was nursing my mother. I didn't have space for much else."

"Don't blame your mother," he said quietly. "According to Belle, she was an unselfish woman. Not the type to make unreasonable demands."

"She *was* unselfish and she did try to persuade me to go out – especially at the beginning when she wasn't too ill . . ."

"But you didn't take her up on it because you were smarting over this Paul character?"

"Oh, you seem to know it all, or think you do!" she blazed, consumed by an anger that swamped the attraction she had felt for him.

"On the contrary, I know only a part of it," his faintly amused smile further enraged her, but before she could speak he went on, "I'd like to know more; the small taste I had yesterday whetted my appetite. Your responses left me in no doubt that you enjoyed it too. However well you may think you can resist me, your sexy body is screaming out for more. It's in your eyes, Katie, you can't deny it."

"You hateful brute!" she threw the words at him passionately, not caring that her raised voice had caused several heads to turn. "You're bad-mannered as well as conceited and – and I wish I'd never had the misfortune to set eyes on you!"

Scraping back her chair she snatched up her bag and jacket and marched outside, her whole being seething with hurt indignation. Damn and blast him! she thought angrily, and didn't look back as she marched away from the restaurant.

Chapter Eight

A FEW people were waiting at the Top Station for the lift and Katrina stood on the fringe, wishing desperately that she could get down the mountain some other way.

The alternative method was by ski-tow, which was out of the question, so she stood, huddled into her jacket, feeling the cold seeping through her boots, which were the fashionable kind and hardly suitable for the snow.

Larry had left the restaurant and was walking towards her, his long legs negotiating the snowy slopes with ease. As he drew nearer and she saw that he looked cool and unruffled, a fresh burst of anger seized her and she turned her back on him, just as everyone began to move towards the lift.

"Come on," he took her arm in a vice-like grip and steered her forward.

"I can manage perfectly well on my own, thank you very much," she said coldly.

"Can you? With these boots? Stop behaving like a spoilt child or I'll pick you up and carry you to the lift."

Knowing that he was perfectly capable of carrying out his threat she allowed him to propel her forward, but once they were seated she tried to keep some distance between them, though the chair was too narrow to make lack of contact impossible.

She was heartily thankful when they arrived back at the car park. If there had been another form of transport, she would have taken it. As it was she was obliged to get into the MG. It was growing dark and the car interior was like ice, but after he had negotiated the mountain road he gave the engine throttle and as they hurtled along she became uncomfortably hot as warm air blasted over her legs.

He had barely uttered a word since leaving the Top Station and she stole a glance at his powerful outline, wondering what he was thinking. Her anger was evaporating, leaving the way clear for other emotions, and she hated herself for being weak enough to wonder if these bittersweet hours spent in his company would be the last.

Of course, they were, she thought miserably. She must not see him again, even if the vague possibility existed that he wanted such a thing. Already he had an unhealthy knowledge of her weaknesses, he seemed to be able to see into her very mind, and the idea of that made her feel uncomfortable.

They were approaching the entrance to the farm and the car skidded a little as he took the turn rather recklessly. Her teeth jarred as he drove the vehicle furiously over ruts and potholes, but instead of going on he slewed violently to the left and brought the MG to a nerve-shattering halt beside a five barred gate. That much Katrina saw before the headlamps were snapped off.

"Satisfied?" his voice was icy. "You spoiled what could have been a perfect day."

She gasped at his audacity. "*I* did! Well, of all the arrogant brutes, you take some beating. You insulted *me*, don't forget."

"I told you the truth, no more, no less."

"You made me sound like a sex-starved flirt! If you think that's true then you're even more of an egotist than I thought."

"That's schoolgirl gibberish and you know it. I was merely trying to point out that you are a warm, responsive, attractive girl who's trying her damndest to prove otherwise."

Katrina met this with silence simply because she could find no argument against it. To contradict him would only give him further fuel and – panic rose in her – it might only serve to make him try to prove his point, so in the circumstances, silence was certainly the best form of defence.

The quietness of the countryside enshrouded them. It was now quite dark and though she could barely see him, she was acutely aware of his closeness.

"Katie," his voice, soft and persuasive, caressed her ears. His hand came over to cup her face, his thumb whispered over her cheekbones.

"I think it might be better if you don't touch me." Her voice came out, shaky and uneven.

The car moved only slightly on its springs as he negotiated the small space between the front seats. She was obliged to make room for him and found herself pinned against the door. "Katie," he murmured huskily before his head came down and his lips claimed hers in a kiss of such sweetness, she forgot her resolve never to respond to him again. Gentleness gave way to something more demanding; she was conscious of a dizzy sensation of desire tingling deep within her. She had never experienced anything like it. Paul had never made her feel like this, so acutely aware of her own body, so alive. A feeling like an electric shock seared through her and all her earlier decisions were swept away in a tide of strange, sweet craving such as she had never known before.

Somewhere in the recesses of her mind a voice clutched at her senses and she remembered a promise to be back at Balgower in time for dinner. She knew it was fast approaching, or perhaps past that time, and she had to struggle out of a desire so deep she had almost forgotten that a relationship with Larry might mean more emotional bruising.

"Larry, I've got to get back."

Her voice brought him to his senses. He moved away from her. The cold night air seeped over her and a chill replaced the deep, pulsating warmth which had so recently embraced her.

"I'm sorry, Larry, I promised Belle I'd be back in time for dinner – and I think I might be late. She and Bob are going out tonight and wanted to start the meal earlier than usual."

He gave a rather unsteady laugh. "Dinner! Of course. You mustn't forget dinner. Despite what you said yesterday I can see you *do* eat though you've just reminded me that you're sticking rigorously to your other sort of diet! Well, you can bloody well choke on it for all I care! I can assure you that I had no intention of seducing you in a sports car just a few yards from Balgower Farm. What

I gave you just now was for starters – an aperitif to whet your appetite if you like. However, I can see you'd prefer to starve yourself of the sort of pleasures other girls take for granted, so we'll leave it there meantime."

Katrina felt as if she had been doused with ice-cold water and was so numb with dismay she was momentarily robbed of speech. Her intention had been to only temporarily forestall him. She had been on the verge of asking him to come over to the farm later. Belle had mentioned that she was going to the Woman's Rural and Bob would be out at a meeting of the Blackface Sheep Breeders Association.

At the time Katrina hadn't minded the prospect of a solitary evening and the idea of asking Larry to keep her company had only just sprung to mind. He had very effectively erased it however with his harsh words. She drew a deep breath and said coldly, "Still flattering yourself, aren't you? I am not your 'other girls' and I have no intention of behaving like them. If, as it seems, all men are like you then I'm better off without them and I'll thank you to leave me alone in future."

He had moved over onto his own seat and before she finished speaking he'd turned the key in the ignition. The wheels skidded on the grass as he rapidly reversed and moved forward at speed. Shakily, she straightened her clothing and pulled a comb through her hair. The gravel chips on the drive spun under the wheels as he brought the car to a halt at the kitchen door.

"I'm flying to London tomorrow with the first chapters of my book," he told her shortly. "I'll be gone for a few days, you'll be glad to know."

Katrina hadn't expected to hear that he was leaving

and she felt utterly dismayed at the prospect. It had been bad enough visualising the long, empty evening that stretched ahead. The play she had intended to watch on television, the good book she had vowed to read in bed, now paled into insignificance. She didn't want to say goodbye to Larry, but she heard herself saying it just the same as she put her hand out to open the car door. The clamping of his strong fingers round her arm stayed her.

"Katie," there was a soft edge to his voice, "I will never force you to do anything you don't want. You must never be afraid of me. I won't ever give you reason to chalk me up as a bad experience. You believe that, don't you, Katie?"

More than anything in the world she wanted to believe the sincerity in his voice and the meaning of his words. His hand came down to cover hers and she turned her head slowly to look at him. The light from the dashboard cast his face into shadow and blurred his outline. She drew her hand away and opened the door.

"Drive safely, Larry," she said, getting out of the car and walking quickly over the gravel chips to the door. The roar of the engine split the night. She watched the receding tail lights flickering among the trees till she could see them no more, then turning, she opened the door and went inside.

The family were sitting round the table and they had a visitor: a large, full-busted lady with iron grey hair and eyes that seemed to swallow Katrina up as soon as she entered the room.

"Sorry we had to start without you, Katrina," Belle

said, by way of greeting. "Yours is keeping hot in the oven but it hasn't been there too long, so won't have spoiled."

"I'm sorry I'm late," Katrina reddened slightly. "I'm afraid I don't have an excuse; we took longer than we thought with our lunch and afterwards we stopped to talk."

Belle's eyes twinkled. "Och, never mind, you're only young once, as long as you enjoyed yourselves that's all that matters. By the way, this is Mrs MacAuley – Winnie to her friends – her husband dropped her off earlier to have a meal with us before we both go off to the Rural."

Winnie MacAuley took Katrina's hand and shook it heartily. "James Cameron's girl, you're like him round the eyes but you've got your mother's colouring. Your father and I went to school together, he was always clever was James and I knew he'd get on in the world. I don't mind telling you, it came as a great shock when I learned he'd been in that tragic accident – and now your poor mother – but from what I hear you did a great job nursing her and if you're anything like either of them, you'll make a go of it."

She went on in her voluble way, probing, cross-examining Katrina about her job, her prospects for the future. "And now you've met Larry Sinclair all over again," her eyes positively gleamed. "*So* romantic. He's a great lad, is Larry, we're all proud of him here, and of course the girls just *adore* him, so you'd better hang on to him like grim death!"

Katrina tried to keep her voice even as she said, "He's going away for a few days, something to do with seeing his publishers, so I don't expect I'll see him again."

"Of course you'll see him again, Katrina," Belle said firmly. "You're here for a while yet, meantime, eat your dinner while it's hot and I want to see the plate cleared."

For the remainder of the meal, Winnie MacAuley did most of the talking. Bob, who had hardly said a word throughout, simply because it was difficult to get one in, exchanged a sympathetic glance with Katrina as he excused himself and left the table to get himself ready to go out.

"I'll wash up," Katrina offered as Belle made to clear away, "I've got the whole evening ahead and will be glad of something to do."

"Are you sure you won't be lonely?" Belle asked. "You could come with us if you like? Though I hardly think it will be your cup of tea."

Winnie MacAuley opened her mouth, but this time Katrina got in there first, "No, thanks, Belle, I'll be quite happy here. There's a play I want to watch and a book I've been meaning to read for ages. You go on and don't worry about me." Scooping a pile of plates from the table she rushed into the scullery with them. Leaning against the sink she took a deep breath and uttered a heartfelt "*Phew!*" as she listened to Belle and Winnie chattering away to one another in the kitchen. She could hardly wait to be alone, even if only to think about Larry and all that had passed between them.

Half an hour later everyone departed into the night; the house was suddenly quiet and empty. Katrina sat by herself in the living room but she didn't turn on the television. It was a relief to just sit there in the silence, thinking of Larry, wondering if she would ever see him again or if he would take her at her word and stay away from her – forever.

Chapter Nine

"KATRINA, phonecall for you."

Belle's voice from the sitting room arrested Katrina as she was halfway up the stairs. It was just before lunchtime on Saturday and she had been at Balgower Farm for a week. She'd spent that morning in the fields with Bob and Jacky, helping them to lift the kale which went towards winter feed for the sheep and two cows that were kept at the farm to supply fresh milk.

Katrina retraced her steps and went into the sitting room to find Belle with the telephone receiver in her hands. Her brown eyes were dancing in the lively way that Katrina was beginning to know well. At this moment there was also a hint of devilment in them and Katrina's steps slowed. She had seen that look before, and it usually meant that something was both pleasing and exciting her father's cousin. "I was just about to take a shower," Katrina said rather warily. "Are you sure the call is for me? I don't know anyone who would be . . ."

"It's for you all right, it's Larry," Belle waved the yellow instrument impatiently. "C'mon, it won't bite." She pushed the receiver into Katrina's hands and went out of the room.

Tentatively, Katrina put the phone against her ear.

"Yes?" She hadn't meant to sound so unsure and she felt both foolish and shaky.

"Hello, Katie, it's me, Larry Sinclair." The deep, cool voice floated down the line and Katrina, feeling a compelling urge to either sit down or fall down, hooked her foot round the leg of a nearby chair and, drawing it forward, sank gratefully into it.

"Hello, Larry, did you have a nice time in London?" she sounded so artificially polite and felt ridiculous.

"Frankly, no, it was hellish," he imparted dryly. "I was bushed when I got back last night and went straight to bed. Listen, I need your help – your professional help – interested?"

His blunt approach put her at a disadvantage. "I'm sorry, I don't know what you mean."

"I'll explain. My publishers like the book, so much so they want it yesterday to coin a phrase. My typing isn't so hot, the two-fingered sort that gets nowhere fast. I've done six chapters of the book, the rest is a mixture of scribbles and tape recorder. A good typist could do the job in a week. Sorry if this is too sudden, I know you've been away from it for a while . . ."

"I did some freelance word processing at home," Katrina was glad that she sounded neither eager nor pushy. "I thought it would be a good way of keeping my hand in."

"Are you game then?" his voice was low and perceptive.

"Okay," she conceded. "I'm sure Belle won't mind me using the sitting room during the day. The television is in here, but if Bob and Belle want to watch it in the evening I'll take the laptop into the kitchen . . ."

"You misunderstand," he broke in impatiently. "We must work together for continuity which means you coming over here every day. What I've said in the tape is a load of rambles. I have to edit it as I go along, so we have to be in on it together for it to work." He gave a short laugh. "Don't worry. It would be a purely business arrangement. I won't force myself on you if that's what's bothering you. When I'm working I tend to forget the world and its distractions. Still game?"

Katrina hesitated, inwardly sweating as she wondered if she could handle the situation. Over the last few days she had barely been able to concentrate on anything. Larry Sinclair had constantly invaded her mind even while she told herself over and over to forget him. But he was not so easily dismissed and she had come to the conclusion that, try as she might, he never would be. The only solution was to put herself in a position of unavailability as far as he was concerned and she had vowed that she would never allow herself to be alone with him again.

Now, here he was on the phone asking her to come every day to his house, his very voice sending shivers up the length of her spine. "When would you want me to start?" she made it sound as if he was her employer and felt so stupid she could have bitten her tongue out.

"Immediately – this afternoon if you can." He sounded faintly amused and she bristled.

"There's the question of transport," she said briskly and was immediately sorry. It was a feeble attempt to stall for time and the anticipated reply came swiftly,

"I'll pick you up of course. It's only a couple of miles along the road."

"No, don't do that, I'll ask Belle if I can use her Mini." She made it sound as if the idea had only just occurred to her.

"All right, I'll hold on while you go and have a word with her." He sounded annoyingly pacifying and her face reddened as she realised that he had probably guessed the Mini was available to her whenever she wanted it. She put the receiver on the table with a definite bang and made the gesture of going through to the kitchen to ask Belle about the car.

"I told you to use it anytime," Belle said warmly.

Katrina, feeling the need to clarify the position, explained that she would be going over to Larry's cottage every day, though she was careful to emphasise that she would be doing so entirely for business reasons. Jacky turned from the sink where he was washing his hands and gave Katrina a knowing wink. "Entering the lion's den," he teased. "Better watch out, Katrina, from what I hear he's an expert hunter and his quarry always consists of beautiful females."

"Och, you be quiet and seat yourself at the table this minute," scolded Belle, though her own eyes weren't lacking sparkle. "Now, Katrina," she chided gently, "I think you know you can use the car as much as you like. If I want to go shopping at any time I'll drop you off at the cottage and Larry can bring you home, so there's absolutely no problem."

Katrina went back to the sitting room and picked up the phone to say briefly, "It's fine, I've got the use of the car."

"Good," Larry sounded pleased then added seriously, "I warn you, it'll be tough. When I get down to work I drive myself to the limit, but in the normal way of things I'm usually the only one involved. You might find me so much of a swine you'll end up hating my guts. Are you willing to take the risk?''

"Yes, I'm willing," she sounded more steady than she felt. "Anything to help an old friend." She smiled to herself at getting just a little bit of her own back. "I'll be over after lunch. Tell me how to get to your place." He gave her concise directions and as she listened she made a little mental map in her mind, hoping all the while that she hadn't missed anything since the very idea of driving to meet him at River Cottage was doing odd things to her thought processes.

They said their goodbyes. Carefully she put the phone back on its cradle and went back into the kitchen where the others were seated at the table and obviously waiting for her. "Oh, go ahead and start," Katrina said rather distractedly. She gazed down at her grubby clothes. "Look at me, I'm a mess. I'll have to shower and change after lunch." She went to the sink and ran water over her hands, gazing ruefully at two nails broken while scrabbling in the earth to free the tough kale stalks. "I pong a bit," she said laughingly, drying her hands and going to draw her chair into the table, "I hope none of you mind."

"None of us smells like a rose garden," twinkled Bob, dunking his bread in his soup without fear of reprisal from Belle who was doing the same. "Besides, there's nothing wrong with the reek of good earth." He glanced at Katrina approvingly, "You were a grand help this morning, lass, you have the country in your blood. It's a healthy life for those that like it."

Katrina remained silent, lost in thought. Her first week at Balgower Farm had flown by and she hadn't yet indulged in any of the pleasant pastimes she'd promised herself. There was so much to do in and around the farm, the days weren't nearly long enough and she had barely given a thought to the city. The idea of going back to her old job was growing less attractive with each passing day and she had pushed it to the back of her mind. She'd phoned her lawyer to see if there was any progress in the sale of the Hampstead house and he had morosely informed her that it was a bad time for house sales. He had sounded jaded and Katrina found herself comparing people she knew who worked in the city to those who worked in the country.

Although Balgower Farm was peaceful, it was anything but dull. The house was never short of visitors and as well as Jacky there was a young boy called Hamish who was training to be a shepherd and another known as 'Speedy', who hadn't yet left school but who spent his spare hours helping Bob with any odd jobs that were going. There was a quality of freshness about them all and Katrina regretted that she had spent so many of her years away from the farm. She had said so to Belle.

"Ach, your father always was a bit of a wanderer," Belle had said indulgently. "He thought it would be good for you to broaden your horizons and that was why he took you abroad. He was wise in his way. There is a time for everything. You might have been bored here when you were a teenager. It's the best time to see a bit of the world and it makes you appreciate the things back home that little bit more."

Katrina sighed a little as she ate her soup. "Jilly thinks

92

the country is deadly," she commented absently, trying
to keep her thoughts on everyday matters so that they
wouldn't stray too far ahead to Larry. She was already
regretting having consented to what he asked but knew
it was too late now to back out.

"Jilly's the girl you're mucking in with, isn't she?"
Belle said conversationally and Katrina gave a burst of
laughter.

"Mucking's the appropriate word. Jilly's idea of tidying up is to shove her things under the bed and sweep the
dirt under the carpet. She's been marvellous, though, I
really appreciated her harebrained way of cheering me
up these last few weeks." Katrina pushed her plate away
and looked in some dismay at the enormous dish of rice
pudding Belle was lifting from the oven. Belle saw the
look and laughed.

"Away you go. You've been like a hen on a hot girdle
since that phone went." .

"Oh, it's not that – it's – I'm not very hungry."

Her protests brought a spurt of mirth from Jacky.
"Can't wait to be swallowed up in the lair! Has Sinclair
affected you that badly, Katrina? If so it might not be a
wise move to be alone with him. He eats little girls for
dinner . . ."

"Oh, for heaven's sake be quiet!" Katrina rounded
on him. "I'm going over there to help him out of a fix,
that's all! I have absolutely nothing in common with him
and I'll thank you to—"

"Hey, hold on," Jacky threw up his hands as if to ward
off a blow, his eyes showing bemusement. "I was only
kidding. I didn't think I was touching a sore spot."

"You talk too much, young man," reproved Belle,

pushing a piled plate towards him. "It's as well you're getting married in the spring. Elaine is just the girl to knock some sense into you."

Katrina felt embarrassment sweeping over her. She had made too much of Jacky's teasing words. Instead of hotly refuting them she ought to have either ignored them or passed them over lightly, instead of which she'd made it plain that Larry Sinclair had got to her – the way it seemed he'd done to many others along the way. "Forget it, Jacky," she said awkwardly. "I'm sorry I shouted. At least you're finding out I'm not the milk and honey type. I've always had to try and control my temper," she ended ruefully.

Jacky had reverted back to his placid self. "I like a bit of fire," he grinned. "Maybe that's why I get along so well with Elaine. She keeps me in my place."

Rather thankfully Katrina escaped upstairs to strip and shower. Fifteen minutes later she emerged, fresh faced and glowing. Belle intercepted her at the foot of the stairs. "There's no need to hurry back, Katrina," she said, tucking away a wilful strand of hair. "You go over to River Cottage and enjoy yourself."

"Belle, I'm not going to enjoy myself," Katrina couldn't keep a note of exasperation out of her voice. "I told you, I'm merely helping Larry out of a fix."

"Oh. I know that – but – you are glad he called, aren't you? This last day or two you've been a bit on edge."

Katrina kept a tight rein on her tongue. "I'll be home for dinner," she said firmly and couldn't help smiling at Belle's somewhat crestfallen expression. "For heaven's sake, Belle, Bob was right about you; you *are* a matchmaker but you're wasting your time as far as Larry's concerned."

"He *is* a very charming man," Belle persisted grimly. "And don't you take any heed of the gossip. People always tend to attach nonsense to handsome men like Larry, but I've known him all his life and can vouch for him."

"No doubt you can," Katrina began to move towards the door. "I'll have to go, Belle, I take it the keys are in the Mini?"

Belle nodded. "Be careful of the second gear, it tends to jump out. Do you know where to go, by the way?"

"Yes, I know." Katrina made a hasty exit, pretending not to see Jacky's smiling face at the window. Belle's words had flustered her and when she got to the bottom of the farm road she found her mind had gone blank and had to sit for a few moments to compose herself and force her mind back to Larry's voice on the phone giving her directions. Nothing like this had ever happened to her before and she felt panic sweeping over her as she tried to recall word for word what he had said. "God Almighty, girl!" she scolded herself aloud. "He's only a man, he can't eat you! Get a grip of yourself!"

She shook herself angrily and guided the Mini on to the main road. The vehicle had certainly known much careless usage. The interior was a clutter of odds and ends of every sort. The heater tube was loose and every jolt of the tortured springs caused hot air to blow willy nilly over various parts of Katrina's anatomy. The second gear jumped out at the most inconvenient times and Katrina was so unnerved she had to exert all her concentration on just driving, leaving none to spare for anything else.

The junction Larry had instructed her to take was on her almost before she realised it and she had to make a rather violent turn to meet it. Almost immediately she spotted a sign that read 'River Cottage' and with her heart in her mouth she guided the Mini up a narrow grassy track which seemed to wind on and on into the hills.

Chapter 10

HALF a mile after leaving the main road she came to a clearing in the glen and there, suddenly, was River Cottage: a sturdy, white, picturesque building standing on a grass-covered plateau that sloped down to a fast flowing river, whose banks were lined with graceful silver birches - so much a part of Speyside. Beyond the house the moors stretched into the misty landscape where summits of snow-covered hills rose ethereally into the clouds.

The MG was parked beside a large barn-like shed a few yards away; its sleek modern lines looking incongruous in the wild splendour of its surroundings. Katrina swallowed hard as she gazed about her. Larry Sinclair had certainly chosen a most remote spot for his hideaway. In normal circumstances she would have been utterly entranced by the sheer beauty of the place, but now the idea of being so cut off from the rest of the world filled her with apprehension.

The door of the house opened and Larry appeared. "Aren't you coming inside? I don't get many visitors in this neck of the woods so it's quite a novelty to have such an attractive one landing on my doorstep."

"I didn't land, I arrived. Somehow or other in Belle's

Mini, I made it; and don't forget, *you* asked *me*, or I wouldn't be here otherwise."

"That's true," he grinned. "And since I was brought up to be polite to visitors, I won't keep you standing out here. Come on in, it's cosy indoors and I've been keeping the teapot warm." Somehow his words made her heart feel lighter. Nothing about Larry Sinclair could be described as ordinary. In fact, he was the most extraordinary man she had ever met. To be near him was an exhilarating experience – yet – with a few well-chosen words he could sound so welcoming and friendly.

The interior of the cottage was wonderfully old-fashioned in appearance, though a glimpse into the small, compact kitchen allowed Katrina to see Larry Sinclair wasn't deprived of the usual modern conveniences. The warmly-carpeted hallway was void of furnishings simply because it was so narrow. But the walls more than made up for it, hung as they were with numerous tiny watercolours of Speyside Valley and some framed photographs of the cottage and its surroundings.

"The den is on your left," Larry indicated a doorway and Katrina went into a homely, cluttered room which smelt of woodsmoke, though the fireplace held only the charred remains of half burnt logs. The fire surround was built from rough stones and looked cheerful with its dressings of horse brasses and other items made of copper. On the hearth stood an ancient, three-legged black iron cooking pot brimming over with logs, another was filled with coal, more logs were piled in a basket in the corner beside a bundle of newspapers and kindling. The huge, deep armchairs were worn but comfortable-looking and two antique tapestry stools were placed invitingly on either side of the fire. Under the window, which looked out on the moors and the hills, stood an enormous mahogany knee-hole desk, full of quaint cubbyholes, its surface almost hidden under a jumble of books, papers and chewed pencils.

Katrina smiled. It seemed that Larry chewed other things besides his nails; it also seemed he was a perfectionist as far as his work was concerned. Discarded notes lay in crumpled balls around the desk and sheets of torn typescript spilled from a wooden waste bucket.

Katrina's eyes were drawn to the walls which were covered with prints of the wild animals symbolic of those found in the Highlands of Scotland. Over the fireplace was a striking painting of an old sailing ship, but it was the array of photographs on the mantelshelf that Katrina found most interesting.

One was of a handsome man and a pretty woman sitting close together on a low drystone wall. Katrina knew instantly they were Larry's parents. She remembered Belle telling her that he and his sister had been brought up by a great aunt and an unaccountable sadness swept through her. He must have lost his parents at an early age; perhaps that was why he was so self-sufficient and able to get along so independently. Another picture was of a young girl with blue eyes and long blonde hair. She looked very like Larry, and Katrina guessed it was his sister, Joan, who was now living in Australia.

A faded photo of a silvery-haired old lady held Katrina's attention. She was dressed in a severe black dress to her ankles and her face was long and hawk-like, though a faint smile quirked her lips. She was vaguely familiar-looking and Katrina realised it must be Larry's great aunt, whom she had glimpsed once or twice from a distance but never forgotten.

Steps echoed up the hall and Larry came into the room bearing a tray, on which was set a fat, blue earthenware teapot, two mugs and a plate of chocolate digestive biscuits.

"Don't stand on ceremony," he said rather sarcastically as she moved away from him to stand by the fireplace. "I'm hardly likely to eat you. Grab a pew and take this while it's hot. It's about the only break you're likely to have all afternoon, so make the most of it."

A fan heater was blasting warm air into the room and Katrina's already warm cheeks grew redder still. "I prefer to stand if you don't mind," she told him stiffly. "I would like to get started as soon as possible because I—"

"Promised Belle I'd be home for dinner," he interposed heavily. He saw at once he had hurt her. She turned quickly away from him, but not soon enough to hide her dismay. "I apologise," his voice, though cool, held a note of persuasive charm. "Especially for the way I behaved the other night. I acted badly, I see that now, but I couldn't seem to help myself. I swear I don't always react like that to women, but since I met you I feel that something big has entered my life. It's scared the hell out of me. I like to be my own master and find it rather disconcerting to know – I'm not."

"Please, don't – don't say anything more on the subject," she said quickly. "I'm here because you asked me to help you and I'll do whatever you want, as long as it's on a strictly business level."

His jaw tightened. "In other words, I can have you for professional purposes but pleasure is strictly out. I've got the message. Loud and clear."

Her fingers tightened around the mug of tea he pushed into her hand. "That was what you agreed to over the phone," she said firmly, drawing her eyes away from his mesmerising gaze.

"Yes, I did," he returned tautly. "And I'm a man of my word, whatever else you may think of me." He continued to stare at her and she tilted her head away from him. The rich red lights in her hair were accentuated in a watery ray of sunlight filtering through the window and his hands curled into balls at his sides. "Shall we start?" he asked curtly.

She put the mug down on the tray and nodded, glad at least that she had managed to maintain her composure for the last few minutes. "The sooner the better," she nodded. "I don't fancy driving back down that road of yours in the dark, especially in Belle's car, I'll never know how it passed its MOT, unless of course things like that don't matter so much in the country."

"They matter, as much as anywhere else. It must be sound enough, despite its looks. Don't worry about going back in the dark, though, I can always take you home; or lead the way, if you'd prefer it."

She bristled at this. "I think I'll manage on my own, thanks just the same. I'll leave while there's still enough daylight to see the way, and I'll have to get used to Belle's car sometime. Practice makes perfect, and I was never the type to avoid a challenge."

"We'll see about that," he said dryly but she felt she had made her point as he turned abruptly and went over to his desk, indicating he was ready to start the afternoon's work.

Chapter Eleven

LARRY proved to be more of a taskmaster than Katrina could have imagined. He was curt and demanding and so distant she felt they might have been miles apart, instead of working alongside one another in the confines of River Cottage.

She was more than relieved to find her typing was as efficient as ever, and as the days passed, she found she was actually thoroughly enjoying typing out Larry's book. It was written essentially to appeal to masculine tastes but there was a sensitivity in the style which she found very attractive and she became so absorbed in the storyline she found herself eager to follow it through to the end. The love scenes were tastefully handled, yet there was such a mix of tenderness and passion about them they touched a chord in her heart and stirred her own heightened emotions to a pitch of longing. The only way to exclude Larry from her thoughts as an exciting and disturbing man had been to treat him merely as a voice dictating to her from a machine.

And very often he was just that. He spent his evenings editing the tapes so that by the time she arrived in the morning, all she had to do was listen and type while he took himself off for long spells, sometimes roaring off in the MG; occasionally going off over the moors on solitary rambles.

She assumed that was the sort of things writers did. He was having difficulty over the ending and went off on his walks armed with pencils and jotters and sometimes a spare tape recorder. Once she glanced up from her work and saw him from the window, his body silhouetted against the backdrop of the moors; his steps carrying him along with effortless ease. In those moments she experienced a great desire to run outside and join him, and she imagined his strong arms opening wide in welcome, his lips on her hair . . .

But she hadn't given in to her impulses. Instead, she forced her mind back to reality. She had made it plain, both to herself and to him, that an intimate relationship was out of the question. Yet, as the days went on, she found herself questioning her own decisions. Seeing him every day was weakening the resolve she had made. She had to admit that he invoked in her a yearning to discover the undreamed of pleasures his mouth had promised. No other man had aroused her in the way Larry had.

Her experiences with Paul had taught her to tread warily as far as men were concerned but they had *not* frightened her away from them as Jilly so often hinted. Circumstances had excluded her from male companionship for a year, but now she was ready to come out and face whatever challenge came along.

Liar! she told herself morosely, her chin cupped in her hands as she gazed broodingly in Larry's direction. Nothing had prepared her for a man like that and she felt a pang of bitterness against him. He had shattered the dream she'd treasured about one day finding a man who would love her unselfishly, who would cherish her for herself and not what he could get from her, and Larry Sinclair didn't fit that category.

She had considered talking things over with Jilly whom she phoned regularly, but something seemed to hold her back. She kept thinking that it would be pointless to discuss a man who had kissed her only twice. In no way could that be construed as a relationship. Jilly would only go on at her about all the things she should and should not do and though Katrina felt older than her friend, Jilly sometimes treated her as if she knew nothing at all about men. She gave the distinct impression of being quite an authority on the subject and Katrina didn't fancy hearing her going on about how Larry should be handled. Anyhow, her feelings were based on too flimsy a structure for them to be brought out and analysed by anyone.

At that point she saw Larry walking up the bank towards the house and she trembled slightly. There was nothing flimsy about this ache of longing she felt for him. It was perhaps as well that he would most likely take himself off as soon as the work on his book was completed. Being near him was a torment and she didn't need that in her life. With a sigh she turned back to the laptop, glad of the diversion that work brought.

Despite the tension, her days at River Cottage flew by and the evenings at Balgower Farm were beginning to bustle with Christmas preparations. The mantelshelf in the sitting room was overflowing with cards and in the corner a fresh green tree glowed with lights.

Belle, her lively face composed into lines of concentration, spent her free time writing out cards and ticking off names from a long, untidy list. Katrina had written and posted off her own cards, nostalgia sweeping over her as she remembered family Christmases, spent in Hampstead or occasionally with friends in Cheshire. She glanced round the homely kitchen. How she wished they had come here as a family during the festive season. There was a special quality of magic about Christmas at Balgower Farm. The fresh holly picked from frosted boughs, fronds of evergreen fashioned into decorative garlands by Belle's nimble fingers, the views of sugar loaf hills, robins in the barn and the animals in the fields; the breathtaking ecstasy of coming into the warm fragrant kitchen from the tingling mountain air. The atmosphere of clock ticking, cat purring, peace was almost tangible and Katrina sighed, thinking it was a shame that people had to drift apart and lose touch. So many experiences were lost, so much left unsaid.

She drew in her breath as a thought struck her. If her parents had continued to visit Balgower Farm she and Larry Sinclair would never have become strangers . . . she propped her chin in her hand and gazed into the fire to dream of how it all might have been; of things that might have happened, words that might have been spoken.

But perhaps Belle had been right in saying there was a right time for everything. She might not have appreciated coming here when she was a teenager. She appreciated it now because it was the right time for it and she felt very fortunate she had been able to turn to people like Belle and Bob when she needed them most. Whenever she felt downhearted there was always something or someone to take her mind off things. Belle was never afraid to say what was on her mind and her direct approach, though often disconcerting and sometimes annoying, was refreshing.

Her curiosity about other folks' affairs was certainly not an unusual trait in a born and bred countrywoman; everyone that Katrina had met so far had this in common. In Belle's case it wasn't just idle prying; she was genuinely interested in the welfare of other people and tried to do her best for everyone who chanced her way. Now there was the happiness of her young guest to consider, and though she tried not to appear too nosy about Katrina's affairs she simply could not help wanting to know more about the things that were going on in her mind.

"How are you and Larry getting on?" she asked one evening as she sat back with her stockinged feet on a stool by the Aga.

Katrina looked up from the book she was reading. Knowing Belle, the question didn't really come as a surprise, but somehow she didn't want to talk about Larry to anyone. "Oh – fine, tomorrow should see the typescript finished," she answered in a noncommittal tone.

"I'm not talking about work," Belle's lips folded meaningfully, and she ignored the warning look Bob threw at her.

Katrina shrugged. "There's nothing else to talk of."

Belle stroked the ears of the marmalade tom on her lap. "Katrina, I'd like to see you settled," she persisted pleasantly. "Now that you no longer have your mother, I feel responsible for your welfare."

Katrina's fingers tightened on her book. "I've no intention of settling yet," she said firmly. "I'm only twenty-two and I intend to have a bit of fun before—"

Her hand flew to her mouth and her hazel eyes widened. "It's my birthday tomorrow! With one thing and another I'd completely forgotten!"

Bob was putting the kettle on for coffee and he looked at her over his shoulder and winked. "Belle hasn't. That's why she's behaving so strangely. She was hoping to herald in your birthday with wedding bells." In the laughter which followed, Katrina forgot the irritation she had felt at Belle's words and went to bed in a happy mood.

Before she left for River Cottage next morning, Joe the Post arrived with cards and a large parcel for Katrina. "Christmas has come early for you, lass," Joe observed, making a few puffing noises and looking pointedly at the teapot.

"They'll be birthday cards," Belle explained as she set a large mug on the table and filled it with thick hot tea.

"Your birthday?" Joe took Katrina's hand and shook it warmly. "Would it be rude to ask how old?"

"She's twenty-three," Belle supplied. "Young enough not to mind being asked.'"

"Twenty-three, eh?" Joe looked at Katrina. "By God! I wish I was that age again. Everything to look forward to, never a care about tomorrow. I bet the lads are queueing up at your door? A bonny girl like you will never go short of admirers."

"No, Joe," Katrina gave a nonchalant laugh, "I'm still footloose and fancy free and intend to stay that way for a while."

"Och, come on, drink your tea," Belle scolded the postman, "you've got no business to be asking Katrina

108

about hers." She eyed the parcel on the table and in the next breath said, "Aren't you going to open it? We're all dying to know what it is."

Katrina's laughter was genuine now and she quickly tore the paper off the parcel, which was from Jilly and contained a Bart Simpson doll with a label round its neck which read, 'Cuddle me in bed till something less spaced-out comes along.' "Trust Jilly," Katrina giggled. "She's like you, Belle, always hinting it's high time I got myself a man. Though, unlike you, I don't think she would consider me experienced enough to deal with someone like Larry Sinclair." Joe looked interested, Belle looked crestfallen, and on impulse Katrina hugged her. "Sorry, I didn't mean that. You've been marvellous to me and I'm being bitchy – but I need time to adjust at the moment and I won't be pushed into any sort of situation involving the things you have in mind for me."

"That's right, lass, you stick up for yourself," Joe nodded, even though he had no earthly idea what they were talking about.

Belle threw him a withering look and accompanied Katrina to the door, which when opened admitted a freezing blast of air into the room. Belle sniffed intently. "I can smell snow, and the hens came down from the trees last night to roost in the barn. They always do that when the weather's going to change."

Katrina pulled a fleecy jacket over the warm sweater she was wearing. It was bitterly cold. The sky was clear blue right to the snowy hill peaks with not a single cloud on the horizon. Waking that morning she hadn't been able to see through the lacy frost patterns on her windows and when she went to feed the hens she'd had to crack the ice in their water bowls before they could drink.

"Mind the roads, Katrina," warned Belle, drawing the lapels of her baggy cardigan across her chest and shivering slightly. "There might be icy patches, it said on the radio there would be." She slid Katrina a sidelong glance. "If it does snow and it gets too bad for driving, don't worry about it – I'll know where you are."

Despite herself Katrina smiled. "Belle, you really are the limit," she rebuked, laughing. "If snow *is* on the way it will be a while in coming and I'll probably be home long before it gets anywhere near making the roads dangerous."

Belle gave her a hug and turned to go back inside, but before the door closed on her she gave Katrina a saucy wink and said pertly, "Give Larry my love, that's if you can bear to share him with anyone else, even an old married hen like myself!"

"*Belle!*" Katrina cried warningly, but Belle had disappeared and only the sound of her laughter could be heard pealing out merrily from the other side of the door.

Chapter Twelve

ON arrival at River Cottage, Katrina found Larry in a slightly more relaxed mood and guessed it was because the book was nearing completion.

There was less than a chapter to type and as she started to remove her jacket she calculated she'd be through by mid-afternoon if she kept hard at it. But after greeting her with a few pleasantries, Larry closed the door of the den and stood against it to look at her.

He was making a great effort to maintain an outward show of calm in her presence and felt his nerves stretching as she began to remove her jacket. Aware that he was watching her, she became clumsy. He hadn't looked at her like that since that day at the Ptarmigan Restaurant. She hoped his long, silent appraisal wasn't an indication of what his mood would be for the rest of the day or she'd never reach the target she'd set herself concerning his work.

The buttons came loose at last and she slipped her arms free, placing the jacket over an arm of the nearest chair. Larry caught his breath and abruptly turned away. "I've perked some coffee," he said shortly. "I thought it would be a good idea instead of tea. If we keep ourselves on top we ought to get finished today."

111

She went to the desk and flipped through some of the pages she'd worked on the previous day. "That's a good idea. Are you – will you be going back to London with the completed typescript?"

"Yes – I phoned Gerry, my editor, a few minutes ago – just before you arrived. I told him if all went well I'd be flying down tomorrow."

"Oh, so you'll miss Christmas in the Highlands?" she spoke as carelessly as she could.

"That depends."

"On – on what?" Katrina's voice quavered slightly.

"On you."

She sat down suddenly on the swivel chair beside the desk. "I really don't see how anything I can say or do should affect you one way or another." She kept her voice calm, but in agitation picked up a pencil and began to chew on the end.

"Oh, for God's sake, let's stop pretending, shall we!" he demanded harshly. "I should think the answer to that is plain. I want to see more of you, Katie, and I know you feel the same – otherwise you wouldn't be chewing the end of that filthy pencil!"

She bent her head. "Look – please, can we talk about it later?" she said in muffled tones. "I'm a typist not a magician, and as well as the end chapter there's a lot of tidying up to be done – so, so I'd be grateful for that coffee."

His eyes blazed and his mouth compressed. "Right," he grated tautly. "I know I should be thankful you show such *overwhelming* anxiety to see the completion of my book, but somehow I don't exactly feel like shouting for joy. I meant it when I told you you've disrupted my life.

This cottage has always been my escape. Now – I'll never be able to come into this room again without seeing you seated at my desk, and because of that I'm bloody well sorry I ever asked you over here! You've helped me get my book finished but you've also destroyed my peace of mind and I'm not grateful to you for that!" He went out, banging the door shut with considerable force.

Katrina worked furiously for the rest of the morning, determined not to allow his outburst to eat into her mind. She heard him outside, chopping logs, the sound of the axe falling again and again. She knew he was deliberately expounding his energy, occupying himself with physical tasks so that he didn't have to spend any time in the room with her. For that she was glad. A situation had arisen between them that she didn't fully understand or know how to handle.

It was almost one o'clock when she sat back and rubbed her aching neck. She was almost there; just a couple more pages to type and some general cleaning up of the typescript. She switched off the laptop and sank into the chair. A strange silence shrouded the room. Larry had stopped chopping. A moment later she heard his footsteps coming up the passage from the side door and she felt her stomach tightening as he kicked open the door of the den and came in, his arms laden with logs.

His hair was ruffled, his face frost-stung. He had obviously worked out his temper on the logs because when he spoke his voice was steady. "I might as well make my last night here a cosy one – even if I'm the only one who'll enjoy it." He set the logs down and, crouching by the hearth, began to roll newspapers into balls which he tossed into the grate.

"Look," she said awkwardly. "You don't *have* to spend Christmas in London if you don't want to. There's absolutely no reason why you shouldn't come back and spend it here . . ."

"Isn't there?" He twisted round and his blue, enquiring stare seared into her. "I should have thought there was one very good and obvious reason."

"I'm-I'm sorry," she stammered. "It may be obvious to you but it isn't to me."

"Damn it, Katie!" His voice was harsher than it had ever been. "Do I have to spell it out to you! I'm damned if I'm going to come back here to just sit and twiddle my thumbs every day. It's up to you to give me a motive for coming back. It's high time you faced the truth. You want me just as much as I want you. It's in your eyes and I want you to admit it to me before this day is over – or, I swear, I'll let you walk out of that door today and you'll never see me again."

"I'll admit to no such thing," she protested hotly.

"No, well can you explain why you're here at all? Surely not because you're brimful of good intentions!"

"You've a damned nerve! You lured me over here on the pretext of our having to work together, yet you've made it your business to be out of the way as much as possible."

"Lured you!" His incredulous laughter was full of sarcasm. "You couldn't get over here quick enough and don't try to tell me otherwise."

She got unsteadily to her feet. "That's unfair and you know it, but now that I see how your mind works I think it's time I went. After all, it wouldn't do to prolong the agony you say exists between us." Her mouth felt so frozen she could hardly get the words out and her legs felt weak as she crossed the room to the door. "Don't try to tell me I'm leaving you in the lurch," she threw at him coldly. "You've had your use of me – I'm sure you're quite capable of finishing what's left of the book."

"Don't be so bloody touchy!" his voice was threaded with remorse. "Stay, for God's sake. I've got to go out, so you can be assured I won't disturb you for the rest of the day."

She was torn between the desire to run out to her car and drive out of his life forever and the equally strong desire to remain and show him that she was strong enough to withstand him. "*Me* – touchy?" she said derisively. "You take some beating for cheek. You're the one who's behaving like a bear with a sore head! Let's just forget it, shall we? We might feel better after we've eaten. I'll go and make something."

She beat a dignified retreat, but once in the sanctuary of the kitchen she looked about her dazedly; so shaken she didn't think she could make a pot of tea, let alone a meal. But he had beaten her to it. He had put sausage rolls in the oven to heat and a pan of tomato soup was simmering on the hotplate. It had been like that nearly all week. He always kept her supplied with tea and coffee and each day prepared simple midday meals. It seemed, as well as everything else, he was a paragon in the kitchen, though she reminded herself he was used to looking after himself at River Cottage.

She put her hands on the drainer to steady herself for a few moments and saw that the sky had grown leaden and the first flakes of snow were beginning to fall. But they weren't settling, and at that moment the state of the weather was the last thing on her mind. Katrina drew a deep breath, then set a place for Larry at the table. She had no appetite but wasn't going to let him see how much he'd upset her. Pouring herself a mug of tea, she put a sausage roll on a plate to carry back through to the den.

For the last six days it had been her habit to eat lunch alone. She knew she'd feel uneasy sitting at the table with him and sensed his relief at being left on his own, though every day he looked at her strangely and thanked her for laying his place.

When he wasn't being brusque, he was unnaturally polite and in a way she was glad this was her last day with him so she could go back to being normal. *Normal!* That was a joke for a start. She doubted she would ever reach that state again. If she was a cataclysm in Larry Sinclair's life, he was doubly so in hers. A tempest seemed to be constantly raging inside her and she felt she would never be calm again.

Larry had left. Her arrival back at the desk coincided with the roar of the MG starting up. A red blur passed the window and she sighed with relief, knowing she'd have the house to herself for a while. She had reached a stage where she found it well nigh impossible to relax when he was nearby.

She drank a mouthful of tea and nibbled at the sausage roll before getting up to go back to the kitchen and switch off the oven. A few dirty dishes were lying in the sink and she washed up, enjoying the peace of the warm, little room with its tranquil view of the foaming river.

When she got back to the den she found it cold. Earlier on she had been uncomfortably hot and had switched off the fan heater and though Larry had lit the fire, the logs were just beginning to crackle. Reaching over, she drew the heavy, wine-red drapes over the window and switched on the angle-poise lamp on the desk. Settling herself in the comfortably padded swivel chair she pushed back her hair and switched on the laptop again, soon absorbed in tapping out the remaining pages of Larry's book. The concluding paragraphs brought a marvellous story to a triumphal ending. She caught her lip; Larry Sinclair was more than just a devastatingly attractive man, he was also a brilliantly gifted writer. Carefully she spellchecked the pages she had worked on that day, making doubly sure everything was correct before saving to disk and printing it out.

That done, she flipped through the last chapters once more, ensnared in the clever twisting and unfolding of the plot; so engrossed with the heroine – whom he had treated with considerable understanding – she forgot about time.

She wished that he could carry his understanding of the female mind through into real life, then she realised that she was being unfair. She had never given him the chance to get to know her better, and now a barrier existed between them that was oddly insurmountable . . .

The sudden opening of the door made her jump violently and whirl round to see Larry, his hair wet, his duffel coat thickly plastered with snow. She felt disorientated. She hadn't heard him come in – come to think of it she hadn't heard his car driving up. A glance at the window showed her it was dark behind the rich wine of the curtains. The afternoon had flown by and she had been so absorbed in Larry's book she had let the fire go down.

He strode over to the hearth and tipped the contents of the coal container into the red hot wood embers.

"I didn't hear you come in," her observation coincided with another: he was wearing only socks on his feet and the toes of them were soaked.

"My shoes got wet," he explained briefly. "I had to leave the car at the bottom of the road and walk up."

"You – you mean the snow is – that bad?"

"Worse, it's drifting. An east wind. You must have heard it when you went through to the kitchen."

"I-I haven't been through – not since you went out."

He glanced at the untouched food and cold tea on the desk. "So I see." He turned on his heel. "I'm going to get out of these wet things and have a shower. Don't let the fire go down. There's plenty of logs."

The reality of the situation struck her with full force. In a desperate bid to pretend to herself it wasn't happening, she picked up her jacket from the chair and began to struggle into it. "I'll have to go," her voice rose, "if I can reach the main road I might make it back to the farm okay."

He faced her, his eyes flashing. "Face it, Katie, you're stuck here with me whether you like it or not. You'll have to stay the night."

"*Where?*" Her voice was a horrified whisper. "I-I mean – where in the house?"

"I would suggest a bed," he snapped impatiently.

"But – I can't – I won't stay!" she quavered.

"Sorry, but there's no alternative," he said disparagingly. "Driving's out of the question, and you'll never make it on foot. It took me all this time to wade through the drifts."

"You shouldn't have allowed this to happen!" she cried vehemently. "Why did you leave it so long to come back? Why did you? Were you driving around with your eyes shut?"

He rounded on her, his jaw clenching, his eyes blazing. "Like a bloody fool I drove to Inverness to get you this!" He withdrew his hand from his pocket and tossed a small, flat package at her. "Happy birthday," his tone was brutally sarcastic. "I had planned to give it to you with a kiss but you're so bloody puritanical you're about as warm as the snow piling up outside. You've been afraid of something ever since you met me and until you face that fact you'll never make it as a woman." He went to the sideboard and, pouring himself a stiff whisky, gulped it down before stalking out of the room.

She stared at the package which had landed on a chair, and drew in a shuddering breath. Her hands were like ice and trembled as she undid the wrapping paper. Inside, nestling in a bed of purple velvet, was a nine carat gold serpentine chain, gleaming in the light.

Her throat tightened. Sinking into a chair she stared at the fire, seeing the orange flames through a watery haze. Picking up the chain she let it slide through her fingers before clasping it round her neck. It felt cool against her skin and she touched it lingeringly. It was beautiful, yet somehow she felt more apprehensive than ever. He had driven all the way to Inverness to get it for her. She swallowed. Something was happening to her she didn't feel strong enough to bear, and Larry Sinclair was the cause of it all.

She heard him moving about in the bedroom across the hall. He came out and went to the bathroom at the end of the passage and there followed the sound of the shower hissing. There was never any shortage of hot water at the cottage because the immersion heater was on continuously. He'd told her the only time the cottage had water problems were if it froze up in winter or dried up in summer.

She heard his whistling above the hiss of steam. His acceptance of the situation made her outburst seem both futile and silly. The domestic sound of running water brought her slightly nearer to reality. Even if the outcome was one she didn't want to face, she would let him see she wasn't a hysterical child. She was twenty-three, for heaven's sake! A grown woman who ought to be perfectly capable of facing anything. She didn't dare let her thoughts wander to the night ahead; instead she forced herself to be calm and practical and to take one step at a time.

Resolutely, she got up and went through to the kitchen to prepare a meal. The larder was well stocked with tinned food and she found cooked chicken legs in the fridge. She put frozen french fries in the oven, popped bread into the toaster, and tossed the chicken legs in batter, and while they were sizzling in a pan, she put meringues into sweet dishes, added fruit cocktail, and topped the lot with whipped cream.

It wasn't exactly the Savoy Grill, rather Speyside

Gamble, she thought flippantly, surprised to discover she was enjoying herself. She had always been good at cooking and it was something of a challenge to concoct a meal from odds and ends. She was about to set the table but decided, no. Trays in front of the fire would be far cosier. It *was* her birthday after all, and she felt like throwing convention to the wind.

She opened the outside door and saw a white world. Great fat flakes swirled and danced in the stream of light; drifts were piling up against the trees. The cottage was effectively cut off from the rest of the world and she and Larry were entirely alone . . .

She quelled her thoughts and shut the door. Larry padded in. He had changed and looked shiny and fresh. She tried not to look at him too searchingly. "Mmm, something smells good," he observed.

"I thought we would have it on trays – do you mind?"

He eyed her quizzically. "You've changed your tune – getting used to the idea of being trapped in the lion's den?"

Ignoring him she turned her attention to the oven to check the chips and flipped the chicken legs over with a pair of tongs. "Look after these, will you?" he was standing just a little too close for comfort and she kept her head averted, "I must give Belle a ring – she'll be worrying."

"She knows where you are – tucked up all nice and cosy with the big bad wolf," his voice was mocking and she flinched.

"You fancy yourself as a quick-change artiste," she said as flippantly as she could. "First a lion, now a wolf. It seems the Speyside forests are teeming with wild animals."

He threw back his head in a spurt of amused laughter and she brushed past him, conscious that he made no effort to step back to let her past. Her skin tingled and she hurried out to the hall where the telephone hung on the wall. A minute later Belle's voice floated down the line. "Hello, Belle, it's me, Katrina. I'm at Larry's cottage and we're snowed in. Thankfully the lines are still up," she was deliberately casual.

"Och, I guessed you would be, dear," Belle sounded faintly surprised. "I told you I wouldn't worry if you didn't make it back."

"Yes, I know that, Belle, but I didn't want you to think I'd left and got stuck in a drift somewhere."

"Katrina," Belle's voice held a note of reproval, "as if Larry would have allowed you to go out in this weather. The main thing is you're snug and you'll be safe with Larry." Katrina drew in her breath. What sort of safety had Belle in mind? she wondered. "Have you got enough food to keep the pair of you going?" Belle's voice took on a note of motherly concern.

Katrina managed to keep her tone even as she said laughingly, "I'm not planning to stay longer than a night."

"It's still snowing, dear," Belle was infuriatingly calm. "And you're very out of the way up there. I wouldn't bank on getting home tomorrow. Why don't you just relax and let your hair down?"

"*Let my hair down!*" the protest was a violent one and Larry, passing at that moment, looked greatly amused.

122

"*Belle*," Katrina dropped her voice. "I'm not treating this as an adventure."

"At your age, you should be. Did you finish the book?" Katrina gave a short account of her busy day and Belle punctuated it with interested grunts. "Now that your work is finished, you can afford to take it easy for a bit," Belle said at last. "Don't worry, you'll be home in time for Christmas."

At that Katrina exploded. "*Christmas!* But that's more than a week away!" Belle's laughter came over the line. Katrina relaxed and laughed too. "You're a rascal, but I love you, Belle Grant," she giggled, and put the phone down.

Chapter Thirteen

THE den was extremely inviting with the firelight flickering on the ceiling, and a tiny lamp on the bookcase
splashing out an orange glow. Katrina sat down on one
of the tapestry stools just as Larry came in bearing an
ice barrel in which nestled a bottle of champagne, packed
round with snow.

"I risked my neck getting this here in one piece," he
said, lifting out the bottle and placing his thumbs against
the cork, which came out with a little pop. "I hope you
don't mind tumblers, we don't run to convention out here
in the wilds," he said as he poured the sparkling wine.

Katrina nodded. "I know, it's rather nice to get away
from it. What are we celebrating?"

He handed her a glass. "The completion of my book
and your birthday. I'm truly grateful to you, Katie, for all
you've done!" He smiled ruefully, "All that fuss and old
Gerry won't get his hands on it tomorrow after all."

"It was a marvellous ending," she said enthusiastically.
"I'm glad you managed to get it right – you were so
worried about it."

He gazed at her steadily. "I wrote the end when I was
just halfway through."

"But – you said . . ."

"Forget what I said. It wasn't true. I told you all that because I needed an excuse to get out of the house. How else do you think I've managed to keep from touching you?"

She lowered her head. "I-I see," she stammered, then rushed on to safer ground. "How did you know it was my birthday?"

His answer was forthright. "I made it my business to find out all I could about you – some I already know—" his eyes narrowed, "a lot more I have still to discover. I find the prospect – exciting."

Katrina put her glass on the hearth and lifted her tray onto her knee. "We'd better eat this before it gets cold . . ." She fingered the chain at her neck. "Thank you for this, it's lovely."

He sat down on the stool opposite and picked up his tray. "Look on it as a consolation for being forced into spending the night with me." She glanced at him quickly but he had picked up his fork and she decided it was safer not to pursue the matter.

They ate in silence. It was very relaxing, with the clock ticking and the snow whispering against the window panes. The meal, though simple, was delicious and they finished off with more champagne. Katrina got up to take the trays through to the kitchen, but decided against washing the dishes. She was beginning to enjoy the evening and didn't want to waste precious time doing domestic chores.

When she got back to the den she saw Larry had piled on more logs and, resuming her seat, she pulled off her boots and wiggled her toes to the luxuriant heat of the fire. She glanced up at the pictures on the mantelshelf and asked him to tell her about the people in them.

His glance followed hers and his face softened. "The one on the left is my parents. My father was a born Scot but my mother was a Norwegian beauty. He was the master of a Merchant Navy cruise liner and he met her on his travels. My sister, Joan, and I were both born in Scotland; my father wanted that. He was very proud of his Scots blood and wanted his children to get to know the place. He couldn't know that we would eventually be brought up and educated in Scotland."

Katrina nodded. "I can't think of a better place. Were you very young when you lost your parents?"

"I was three and Joan eight. Ironically they drowned in a sailing accident."

Katrina bit her lip and said quietly, "And the old lady – she's your great aunt, isn't she?"

"Was," Larry corrected, a reminiscent smile hovering on his lips. "She looks a real old dragon but she had a heart of gold and the constitution of an ox. She needed both to take a couple of youngsters into her home and bring them up as her own. All this—" he glanced round the room, "—came from her croft. It might not fetch much in a saleroom, but to me it's priceless."

Katrina was intrigued and felt she had to know more about him. "I know your sister lives in Australia, but you – where do you live when you aren't here?"

"You could say out of suitcases. I have a pad in London and spend my time there when I'm not travelling – I think I like it here best though. I feel this is where my true identity lies."

"I can understand that," she said softly. 'And, of

course, if one is creative it's ideally situated." She gazed dreamily into the fire, "I know it's hard work being a writer but – it must be exciting too."

"Only in short bursts," he said dryly. "Sometimes I think I might have been better off if I'd stayed in the Merchant Navy, but of course I say that with tongue in cheek."

"You followed in your father's footsteps then?" she ventured, and Larry looked up fondly at the picture of the sailing ship above the fireplace.

"The sea is in our family's blood. I joined when I was eighteen. That's when I got the travel bug and also the urge to write more. I started to scribble seriously on my first trip. My earliest novel was centred on Trinidad and only accepted after a flood of rejections. I couldn't believe it when it proved to be a hit. I've written a dozen or so since then – on average, one a year." He got up to tip more champagne into their glasses. His hand brushed against hers as he said lazily, "Now – what else can I tell you about myself that you haven't yet managed to wheedle out? My hobbies are fast cars, beautiful women, and travel – not necessarily in that order." He was being facetious but she couldn't help responding to his unrepentant grin.

"My father was like yours in a way," she said uncertainly, feeling that she had to keep the conversation on safe levels. "He left Scotland early and went to London to become a civil servant. He met my mother on holiday abroad. She was a Londoner, and they always joked about how they had to go half-way round the world before bumping into one another. They loved to travel – that's why I didn't get the chance to come to Scotland more often. Mum worshipped the sun and we went to France a lot."

"Pity," his narrowed gaze was still on her and she shifted uncomfortably. "But for the Scottish weather we might have come together sooner."

"We-we might," she agreed unwillingly, wishing the conversation hadn't come round to personal levels. She had never been more aware of any man than she was of him. She was conscious of every little move he made, yet in the past half-hour she felt lulled into a state that bordered on tranquillity. Even so, she was aware it was a false sense of security. She hadn't wanted any of this to happen, but due to unforeseen circumstances, it most certainly *was* happening. She glanced at him and wondered if an affair with him might rid her, once and for all, of the humiliating memories of her relationship with Paul. Larry was so different in every way: he had pride and dignity and he had proved to her that he was able to resist his own sexual impulses with a strength of will that appealed to her. Perhaps if she allowed herself to meet him half-way, it might do wonders for her peace of mind . . .

She almost laughed aloud. Since meeting him there had been *no* peace of mind. She was nervous and edgy all the time, alternating between apprehension and anticipation, and she was frightened of the passion he had awakened in her. He'd said she was a puritan and afraid. Perhaps he was right. But afraid of whom? Of him? Or of herself?

"What did Belle have to say about your spending the night with me?"

The suddenness of his question caught Katrina unawares. "Oh, she said I wasn't to worry."

129

"And are you?"

"Am I what?"

"Worrying?"

Katrina lowered her head. "N-no. Why should I be?"

"Because you're afraid of the situation we're in. It's very intimate, isn't it, Katie? You and me, snowed up together in a Highland cottage – intimate and romantic. If you let yourself go you might discover a whole new aspect of Katrina Cameron you never knew existed."

"I don't know what you mean."

"I mean this: Paul Carrington stifled you. It's my guess you met him at a time when the real woman in you was just starting to emerge, only he was the sort of selfish bastard who thought only of himself. Instead of bringing you out, he pushed you back into yourself. Am I right?"

She shivered, despite the fire's heat. "Put like that – I-I can only say it's no wonder you're a writer."

His fist crashed down on the arm of his chair. "For Christ's sake! You've become such an expert at evading the issue you won't bloody well face up to it when it's spelled out to you!" He banged his glass down and got up to stride over to her with the champagne bottle in his hand. Tipping it up he poured the remainder into her glass till it was brimful. Pushing it towards her he ground out, "Drink that! With any luck it might help to loosen you up a bit!" He was big and looming and somehow terrifying and her hand shook so much her drink spilled over, soaking her jeans. She jumped up and ran out of the room to the kitchen where she seized a towel and mopped frantically at the stain.

130

Larry came in behind her and stood watching in amusement. "I suggest you take them off," his voice was heavy with calculated patience. "Take everything off and allow yourself to relax. I'll give you a dressing gown to cover your modesty."

"I'll take you up on that offer," she threw back at him furiously. "In fact, I'm going to have a hot bath and then I'm going to bed – *on my own.*"

His eyebrows rose in a show of surprise. "Suit yourself," he said wearily. "I'll say this for you, you're frank to the point of being brutal – you've also shown me you have fire in your veins, and I like a woman with spirit."

He went out of the room but came back in minutes with a towelling robe which he pushed at her. "I'm sorry I can't run to pyjamas," he told her with a slight smile. "I never wear them. If you keep this on in bed you should be warm enough."

She clutched the dressing gown to her chest and with head high, marched out of the kitchen and along to the bathroom – a fair-sized room with a modern suite and corner shower unit. While the bath was filling she stepped out of her jeans and took them to the sink to immerse the stain in cold water. She wasn't sure if that was the correct method for removing wine, but by then was beyond caring and hung the garment over the hot rail together with her underwear.

The bath was blissful. She lay back, feeling the tension slowly ebbing from her limbs. She closed her eyes and listened to the wind keening over the moor. She could hear Larry moving about and her feelings of unease returned with full force. Fool that she was!

131

In her anger and confusion she had omitted to ask him just where she was supposed to sleep. She knew there were two bedrooms and she consoled herself with the thought that he was probably getting the spare ready now. She was unwilling to leave the comfort – and more importantly the safety – of the bathroom but knew she couldn't lie in the bath forever. After twenty minutes she reluctantly climbed out and enveloped herself in a big, warm, fluffy towel from the hot rail. Remote as River Cottage was, it certainly wasn't lacking in comfort. The shaggy bathroom carpet was luxurious and she curled her toes into its pile as she dusted herself from a big tub of talcum powder. It was cool against her skin, and she smiled a little as she realised it was a brand reputed to drive girls wild. One thing was certain, Larry Sinclair achieved that very successfully without having to rely on anything that came out of a tin.

She wriggled herself into the robe. It was miles too big for her but once she'd rolled up the sleeves and tied the loose folds round herself, it wasn't all that bad. Running her fingers through her hair she made a face at herself in the steamy mirror before opening the door to peep into the dimly-lit hall, wondering to herself if he had already gone to bed and if he was in his own room – or the spare!

Chapter Fourteen

"YOU can have my room, I've changed the bed."

She hadn't expected to hear his voice at such close quarters, and as her heart hammered in her throat she was sure he must have heard her startled intake of breath.

He was standing just along the hallway, a tall dark silhouette in the soft light from the den. His arms were full of pillows and she guessed he must have come from the linen cupboard just outside the bathroom.

She drew herself up and said as calmly as she could, "Please – don't put yourself out for me."

He sighed. "Don't fuss, I've already done it. The spare room hasn't been aired so I've taken the mattress out and put it in the den. I've done it before on really cold nights and I've got a good sleeping-bag and plenty of blankets, so I'm hardly roughing it."

She came towards him slowly, halting a little distance away. "Larry," her voice was soft, "I've – I've enjoyed this evening . . . Some of it, at least."

"So have I." He appraised her silently. In the dim light her face looked pale, her hair very dark, the robe swamped her but only served to heighten her femininity. "Pity it had to end."

She nodded. "Yes, I'm sorry I behaved so foolishly tonight – it's just—"

"—that you're a nice girl."

Colour flooded her face. "Please," she whispered, "don't say it like that."

"Why not? You *are* a nice girl and I'm the one who should apologise for being so blunt. I respect you for what you are and because of that I'm not going to attempt to get you to go to bed with me, though we both know I could do it quite easily if I really wanted to." Katrina swallowed hard and said nothing. "I think we ought to say goodnight," he continued. "I won't say it with a kiss," the mocking note in his voice made her feel utterly miserable, "as I couldn't promise that it would stop there, so, like a perfect gentleman, I'll allow you to go untouched."

Blindly, she turned from him and, going into his bedroom, she shut the door and stood with her back to it. She felt no triumph at having successfully evaded him; rather she was overcome with such overwhelming frustration she felt weak. She had just spent the most stimulating evening of her life and allowed it to end in a complete anti-climax.

He had called her 'a nice girl'. Oh God, he must think her naïve! She had behaved like a sixteen-year-old schoolgirl instead of a grown woman of experience. Experience! That was a good one! She wasn't experienced , that was the trouble. Her early sexual adventures had scarcely made her liberated. She had believed that would come with Paul's entry into her life and had high expectations of how such a man would treat her. He'd given every indication of having the experience she lacked, and she'd looked to him to show her the way.

She laughed mirthlessly. What a child she'd been. He had soon shattered her immature dreams and robbed her of her romantic illusions. How she must have flattered his ego with her eagerness to be seen in his company, and her desire to please. At first she hadn't known any better and it had thrilled her to be taken to expensive nightclubs and restaurants. She'd been dazzled by the glitter, completely taken in by his charm. But under the handsome veneer he had been shallow, selfish and astonishingly vulgar, and she doubted that any girl could find fulfilment with a man like him. She was thankful now that he'd walked out of her life when he did, though at the time she'd been hurt because she truly believed that he would change – that she had the power to help him do it . . .

Katrina sat down on the edge of the bed and took stock of the room. It contained good, solid, old-fashioned furniture which she guessed came from Larry's child-hood home. On the cabinet, an amber coloured bedlight gleamed warmly on the lovely old brass of the bedhead and splashed over the thick cream pile of the carpet. Part of a sock and the sleeve of a blue jersey protruded from a drawer and she smiled despite herself. He had obviously made a quick tidy up of the room while she'd been in the bath.

She got up and wandered over to the bookcase to run her fingers over a collection of C. S. Forrester's sea adventure novels. She imagined Larry relaxing in bed with one of his favourite stories. She pictured him in this room, just pottering about as he prepared for bed. *Larry. Larry. Larry . . .*

She couldn't get his name out of her head. Without being able to help herself she went over to the dresser and, taking the sleeve of his jersey in her hands, she savoured the feel of it and shivered as a wave of overpowering longing washed over her. She couldn't pretend any longer. She wanted him more than she had ever wanted anyone in her life before. She wanted him to make love to her; she was hungry for the touch of his lips on hers and she wanted him to know that she wasn't the puritan he imagined her to be – that warm blood flowed in her veins. That her being was diffused with emotions so powerful she was no longer in control of them – he was their master and she had to let him find that out for himself.

But how? *How?* she asked herself in torment. She couldn't very well go to him now after warning him off so successfully.

She paced relentlessly, her bare feet padding soundlessly on the carpet.

Then with an impatient shrug she snatched a book from the case and pulled back the patchwork patterned duvet, only to stare in dismay at a smouldering patch on the sheet. Oh no! she thought in panic. He had switched on the electric blanket and it had either been left on too long or there was a fault in the wiring.

She wasn't the sort to easily lose control. She'd been used to dealing with all kinds of minor emergencies nursing her mother, but the complexities of electric wiring weren't within the bounds of her knowledge and she hesitated only fractionally before running to the door to wrench it open.

Larry was just coming out of the bathroom. He had undressed and was wearing a robe similar to the one he'd given her. "Larry," she kept her voice even, "I think there's something wrong with the electric blanket. It's smouldering."

A few quick strides took him into the room and in minutes he had the situation in hand. "I'm sorry, my fault," he ran his fingers through his hair. "I'll have to re-make the bed," his blue gaze defied an answer and she held her breath as he added, "unless, of course, you wish otherwise."

They contemplated one another for minutes that seemed to stretch to eternity. He took a step nearer and instinctively she crossed her arms over her chest. "That – would be a bit much to ask." She was unable to tear her gaze away from his. "We've both had a rather harrowing day, and you must – you must want to get to bed."

He came closer still. "Very much. Do you?"

She felt the breath squeezing from her lungs. "Yes, I think I do – I'll – go and get a fresh sheet." But before she could make a move he covered the short distance between them and his hands slid round her waist to pull her close in against him. Katrina trembled as she saw the expression of desire in his eyes, her heart seemed to stop beating entirely before it went racing on. He was looking at her face as if he couldn't get enough of it.

"Katie—" he murmured huskily before his hands came up to cup her face and he bent his head to brush her lips in a kiss both tender and loving.

His hands came round to bring her body closer to his but there was no need, she melted against him and gave herself up to the ecstasy of being in his arms. His mouth was firm and fresh on hers and helplessly she gave in to him as shivers of delight went through her. She could feel the tension leaving her limbs and she allowed herself to relax. When his hands slid inside her robe she made no protest, her skin tingling as his fingers caressed the creamy skin of her shoulders and tangled into the damp tendrils at the nape of her neck. His breath was coming faster and she was amazed she could have this effect on him.

"Katie, you're beautiful," he whispered. "I was going crazy out there in the den – knowing that you and I were under the same roof. Katie—" his breath came out in a sigh as he crushed her to him once more. Again and again they kissed, each one deeper than before. A shaft of fire seared through her, his hands were moving expertly over her body and she gave a little moan . . .

He was bringing her to the sweet delirium of some unknown summit and she clung to him with unashamed passion. There was no turning back now, Larry's body was becoming more urgent, his eyes were dark with desire, his mouth was hard and demanding against hers.

"Let's go to bed," he suggested at last. She nodded and allowed him to lead her through to the den where he gazed at her for one long moment before pushing the robe from her shoulders. It fell in a heap to the floor. "Don't be afraid," he whispered into her hair, "I won't do anything that you don't want me to."

He had placed the mattress near the fire and the silky

material of the sleeping-bag was warm against her back. She watched as he shrugged himself out of his robe and lay down beside her. After that she forgot everything. All the warmth and passion she could ever want was here, in this room, in this house, in the arms of Larry Sinclair who had, at last, made her feel the complete woman she had always wanted to be.

Chapter Fifteen

KATRINA uttered a sigh as she slowly emerged from a deep and satisfying sleep. She moved her unfettered limbs, revelling in a sense of complete freedom as she lazily stretched both arms over her head and turned on the pillow without opening her eyes.

A feeling of satisfaction pervaded her entire body and for several moments she remained as she was, warm and contented. Hazily she wondered at the absence of sounds she'd come to associate with early mornings at the farm.

The delicious fragrance of frying bacon assailed her nostrils and she wondered why Belle wasn't singing and clattering the dishes and why the hens weren't clucking in their usual happy fashion as they poked among the chaff left over from the last feed. The sound of a motor filtered though the silence which meant Bob or Jacky had started up the tractor.

A frown creased her brow and then, as the memory of the previous night came flooding in, she caught her breath and became fully awake; instinctively gathering a blanket around her before sitting up to reacquaint herself with her surroundings and get her thoughts into focus.

The bed was rumpled, the blankets in disarray, and

she looked down, expecting to see Larry at her side, but the space beside her was empty, and she became aware of vague domestic sounds from the kitchen. The curtains were still drawn but the dazzling white countryside threw back its light and everything in the room was plainly visible. The ashes in the grate were white and dead but the den was pleasantly warm and she realised the gentle whirring she had attributed to Bob's tractor came from the fan heater over by the desk.

Her attention was arrested by the sight of her robe lying on the floor and warmth diffused her being at the memory of Larry taking it off. Reaching over, she pulled it round her shoulders, shivering a little as the cool material touched her flesh. Her fingers went to the chain at her neck and she played with it absently, her heart quickening as she thought back to Larry's lovemaking. He had carried her with him to pinnacles of deepest pleasure which she had felt couldn't be surpassed, but in the early hours of morning their passions had erupted anew and hungrily they had made love once more.

The memory weakened her limbs and she lay back on the pillows, an uneasiness seizing her. For over a year now she had been the mistress of her own emotions; she had built a barrier round her heart and though it had been a fragile one it had provided her with a certain measure of protection. Larry had very effectively brought all her defences tumbling down and the feeling of being exposed to all the hurt an affair with him might bring was not entirely welcome.

The experiences she had shared with him completely swamped all that had gone before; her memories of Paul were fragmentary, flimsy images so transparent she could hardly remember what he looked like now. She shuddered. There was danger in that somewhere. Larry was all powerful, filling her vision with everything that was warm and real, and if she didn't want to get bruised again she simply had to keep a certain distance between them – this had been just an interlude in both their lives, something that would never happen again . . .

The door opened and Larry came in. Without looking at her, he strode to the window to pull back the curtains. Katrina saw the sky was a deep blue and smiled when she saw a blackbird in the topmost branches of a spruce tree, looking most unconcerned as the wind swayed it about.

Larry came over to the bed and without hesitation, crouched down. Taking her in his arms he kissed her deeply. He smelled of soap and toothpaste and she put out a finger to trace the line of his jaw. He seized her hand and nuzzled the tips of her fingers, his thumb probing her palm with an intimacy that sent a stab of response through her veins.

He released her hand and stood up quickly. "If I touch you I can't promise you'll see the light of this beautiful morning – besides," he smiled, "all my culinary efforts will have been wasted. Bacon and eggs on the table in five minutes and that's an order."

"My clothes!" she laughed. "Hadn't I better put them on?"

He made a face. "If you don't I won't answer for the consequences." He went out of the room and she scrambled up to run to the bathroom. Her underwear was dry and she washed herself quickly before dressing, only to discover that her jeans were still wet. Blast! she thought, still smiling a little as she visualised herself padding about the house wearing only a jumper over her tights. Wrapping herself once more in the robe she went to explain the situation to Larry. He rummaged through his things, eventually coming back with a pair of his own jeans.

"You can roll up the legs," he told her. "Hardly the latest fashion but it doesn't matter here and as you'll be wearing a pair of my wellies later you'll look quite stunning."

There followed one of the most wonderful days Katrina had ever experienced. It was a crisp, clear morning with the sun sparkling on the snow and glinting on the river. The distant hills were languorous, with blue shadows lying in the snow-filled corries and on the dazzling reaches of the moors.

Larry had suggested packing a picnic lunch. This they did together before going off to explore the moors, keeping to a sheep track that wound its way upwards. Although the snow was thick it was crisp and firm in the higher altitudes and they were able to move along reasonably well.

A good stiff climb later they paused for a rest and sat side by side on a rock, looking back at the way they'd come. The chimneys of River Cottage were prodding up through the trees, the river glinted far below. "We came here once, you know," he said, holding her hand as he spoke.

"Did we? I don't remember."

"You were just a nipper," he laughed. "There's a lot you probably don't remember. There was quite a little gang of us that day – you included – and we set off on bicycles and landed up here. It was summer, we brought food and tins of coke. We paddled in the river then climbed up here. You snagged your shorts and scratched your knees on bramble thorns. You were always doing things like that. We were all fascinated by the cottage. It was empty then and we looked in the windows and I said that one day I'd buy it and live here."

She stared at him as, very gradually, a memory stirred in her. "I *do* remember now, just snatches; it's so unfair, you being able to talk about things I've forgotten."

"That five years between us made a lot of difference. Strange, isn't it? The twists of fate? I never dreamed in those days that I'd become a published writer and have enough money to buy River Cottage. Now . . ." his fingers stirred in hers, "even better things are happening. I've met you all over again, and I hope you won't slip away from me so easily this time."

"I have a job to go back to," she reminded him. "My life is in London."

"We're both in a similar situation, and I'm sure we could work something out. We'll see each other in the city; we can come here for holidays – you can help me write my books so we have enough time to spend together."

At his words her heart began to sing and she giggled, "You've got it all worked out, haven't you? Right now I'm starving, let's get the food out and eat, all this fresh air has given me the appetite of a horse."

When they got home later that afternoon they put extra food out for the birds and scattered nuts for a red squirrel who chattered at them from the branches of a Scots pine. After that they had a snowball fight and built a large snowman, giving him a carrot for a nose and bits of coal for his eyes.

Scanning the landscape with binoculars they spotted a herd of red deer searching the moor for food, and Larry fetched a bale of hay from the supply he kept in the barn. Tying it on to a piece of corrugated iron they pulled it away from the cottage and spread it out in a clearing among the trees.

Towards evening Larry built a huge log fire in the den and then they went into the kitchen to make dinner. Afterwards, when it was eaten, and the dishes cleared and washed, they went back to the den and Katrina settled herself against his knees; her hands clasped round her legs.

Though they chatted easily, Katrina was aware of a growing sense of anticipation inside her. He had begun gently massaging her neck and although she loved the feel of his strong fingers on her skin she also experienced a pang of unease.

She felt she was too happy for it to last. Whatever happened, she *mustn't* let herself fall in love with him. He had told her quite frankly that women played an important part in his life and by giving in to him, she had allowed herself to be chalked up as another statistic. She knew it was rather a cynical view but the idea appalled her. She had already asked herself how many women he had taken to bed. She could hardly bear to think of someone else lying in his arms and impulsively, as if to claim him for her own, she melted further against him, closing her eyes as he played with her hair and trailed his fingers over the top of her spine.

For a few minutes more she let herself enjoy his touch then she said with a sigh, "I suppose I ought to give Jilly a ring. She'll be wondering why she hasn't heard from me."

"Jilly?" he asked questioningly.

"Yes, Jilly Watson. I'm sharing her flat till I find a place of my own. We've been friends since secretarial college and we were lucky enough to get jobs in the same place when we left. She's a blue-eyed blonde with strings of boyfriends."

"Jilly Watson," he sounded thoughtful and Katrina twisted round to look up at him.

"You sound – almost surprised," she frowned a little, "as if you know her?"

He regarded her through narrowed lids and said easily, "Let's just say I know – or have known, a few Jilly Watsons in my life."

"Yes, you did say women were a hobby with you." She hadn't meant to sound so resentful and she turned quickly from him to gaze into the fire.

"You're fishing," he sounded amused. She refuted the statement too vehemently and he laughed. With a flick of his wrists he pulled her up onto his knee to look defiantly into her eyes. "For God's sake, Katie!" his mouth twisted ruefully. "I'm almost thirty and hardly bloody celibate if that's what you mean! Of course there have been women – mainly one night stands; one or two slightly longer. I took what was offered me and if I sit here and tell you otherwise I would be lying. Don't tell me you're jealous?"

She opened her mouth to protest but his lips came down, smothering her words, sweeping away all her anxieties. It was as if she couldn't get enough of him. She forgot Jilly, she forgot everything except the rapturous sensations invoked in her by his masterful lovemaking.

Chapter Sixteen

REALITY filtered back into her world sometime in the dark hours before dawn. The steady, unmistakable sounds of a thaw penetrated her consciousness and swept away the remnants of sleep. The snow was sliding off the roof and running through the gutters. Her heart sank. The dreamlike idyll with Larry was over.

In the beginning she hadn't wanted it, but now she didn't want to escape the confines of River Cottage and Larry Sinclair. The romance of it couldn't be denied; the happiness she had shared with him couldn't be dismissed lightly, yet her more practical senses warned her it couldn't last.

She had to accept the encounter owed itself to circumstance and it was over. She looked at Larry asleep by her side. His fair head was tousled, his rebellious mouth relaxed. Everything about him suggested strength and warmth. She tore her eyes away from him. She mustn't think like that. Larry Sinclair was an essentially powerful man in every way and to see him in any other light was stupid as well as self-destructive. She couldn't risk becoming involved with him. A strong physical attraction existed between them, that was all.

When Christmas was over, everything would go back

to normal and he would go his own way and forget all about her. Quite suddenly normality seemed to her the dullest state on earth. He might forget her but she would most certainly never forget him. He had changed everything in her life. For twenty-three years she had believed herself fully alive, but not until meeting Larry had she been truly awakened and she could never forget someone who had made her so aware of her own body. The idea of allowing another man to do the things that Larry had done was beyond her comprehension. She bit her lip. She couldn't look that far ahead. She had to take one step at a time.

She lay by his side until dawn filtered weakly through the curtains, then she got dressed and went through to the kitchen to open the outside door and look out. It was raining; a steady, persistent drizzle which was effectively washing away the snow. The snowman that she and Larry had so carefully made was collapsing bit by bit, and looked as dejected as she herself felt. The Mini, looking like a huge lump of icing sugar, was still up to its wheel arches in a drift, and Katrina realised that they would probably have to walk down to his car at the foot of the track.

They set off just after eleven. Now the time of departure had come, Larry seemed anxious to be off. He had phoned Dalcross Airport, to be told that the runway was clear, and had proceeded to pack a weekend bag with a few necessities. He discarded the casual clothes Katrina was used to and instead wore a more formal jacket and shirt.

Before leaving the cottage he reached for her, and

without a word he pulled her into his arms and sought her mouth. Katrina tried not to respond, instinctively preparing herself for the empty days that stretched ahead. His lips caressed her ear and she trembled, hating herself for her own weaknesses.

"Please, Larry, we'd better go," she said, but there was no strength behind the words. She leaned against him, savouring his nearness, yielding her mouth to his. She wanted to cling to these moments for as long as she could and when at last he reluctantly pushed her away she felt strangely bereft.

At the last moment he remembered the typescript and as he stuffed it into a folder and packed it away they both laughed a little, though in Katrina's case it was half-hearted. At the door he donned wellingtons and his duffel coat for the walk down to the car, and despite herself Katrina smiled at his feet encased in the large boots.

"Just for that you can carry my shoes," he said with mock severity, thrusting a brown paper bag into her arms. His arm slid round her waist, pulling her in close, and silently they trudged down the slushy track. Katrina didn't look back at the cottage and she was glad when the snow covered shape of the MG came into view.

Larry cleared the windows and unlocked the doors before changing back into his shoes. He shrugged himself out of his coat and tossed it and the wellingtons into the back of the car. He looked at Katrina for a long considering moment and she felt her nerves stretching, wondering what he was thinking.

"I should be back in time for Christmas." He spoke the words casually.

She nodded. "Yes."

"Try and behave yourself till I get back."

"Larry," she began hesitantly, "you mustn't think—" she swallowed, unable to go on.

A frown darkened his brow. "I mustn't think what?"

She wanted to tell him that the intimacies they'd shared at the cottage weren't an indication of how she intended to go on, but the words stuck in her throat and she couldn't meet his quizzical blue stare.

He flipped the car keys into the air and jingled them in his palm. For a few more seconds he regarded her musingly then, without speaking, pointed to the passenger seat.

She got in, shuddering at the harsh banging of the door. She thought he was angry but when he came round to fold himself in behind the wheel, his face gave nothing away. He inserted the key in the ignition and the engine turned sluggishly once or twice before firing into throaty life.

Although the road was rutted with gritty slush, driving conditions were fairly good, and the two-mile journey to the farm was achieved in a very short time. The farm track was a different story, but despite Katrina's protests she could walk the rest of the way, he ploughed on, slithering and sliding but somehow keeping going till they arrived at the yard in front of the house without mishap.

Larry didn't say goodbye. Briefly, his hand touched her hair before he turned away, his demeanour indicating that he wished to be off. She barely had time to shut the passenger door before the MG's wheels spun impatiently and he drove speedily away.

She composed herself for a few moments before entering the house, hoping that her face didn't give too much away. It was strange, but she felt so different inside she was certain it showed. Only two days had elapsed since she had last been at Balgower, but so much had happened it seemed as if she'd been gone for considerably longer.

She had no time to think about anything more. Belle was at the door, her lively face expressing delight even before she spoke. Two of the cats came out to wind themselves round Katrina's legs and in an odd way she felt that she'd never experienced such a genuine welcome home.

Belle propelled her inside and, sitting her down at the table, smiled at her with dancing eyes. "The place has been dead without you and that's a fact," her glance took in Katrina's reddening cheeks. "But I can see your break has done you good." Katrina bent down to pull off her boots, her hair falling over her face. She might have laughed if she hadn't felt so embarrassed. Belle was no fool, she must have guessed things had happened at River Cottage, yet she was talking as if Katrina had just returned from a Sunday school outing.

Katrina straightened. "My break?" she said incredulously. "Belle, you surely don't *condone* what has happened?"

Belle stood with the kettle suspended in mid-air looking thoughtful. "Well, dear," she said at last. "I don't feel qualified to pass my opinion, but if you really must know I can only say it had to happen sooner or later and I can't say I'm sorry it happened with Larry."

Katrina was half amused, half exasperated. "Oh, Belle,

am I really such an open book? Can everyone read me so easily?"

Belle poured piping hot water over instant coffee and spooned sugar into large mugs before answering. She slid Katrina a sidelong glance. "Not everyone, Katrina, only folks really close to you. This last week or two I've felt as if I had a daughter about the place and I've come to know you pretty well. If you want the truth, I'm glad Larry was here to take your mind off things. Your mother would have approved of him, I'm sure, and she'd be pleased to know he's helping you to enjoy your holiday in Scotland."

"He's certainly doing that," Katrina murmured faintly.

Belle ripped open a packet of tea biscuits and scattered the unbroken ones onto a plate. "Is he coming back for Christmas?"

"I think so – yes, he did mention that he would be."

Belle positively beamed. "Good, we'll have a party. If we clear the sitting room there ought to be space for about fifteen. How about Boxing Day?"

Katrina's mouth twisted wryly. "Anything you say, Belle. There's more to you than meets the eye. You have quite a knack of getting things to move in the direction you want."

Belle pulled an innocent face. "I don't know what you mean, Katrina. Now, drink your coffee while it's hot and we'll sit with our feet up for ten minutes while we discuss arrangements."

"Arrangements?"

"For the *party*! Really, dear, your mind *is* far away – oh, while I remember, that friend of yours – Jilly –

phoned last night. I told her you were in the bath and would ring her another time."

Katrina stared. "Why on earth did you tell her that?"

"I couldn't very well tell her the truth, could I?" answered Belle reasonably. "Besides, she does sound a bit nosy and I thought if you wanted her to know anything you would tell her in your own time."

Katrina burst out laughing. "Belle Grant, you're a diplomat! Let's get a space cleared and we'll make out lists for this grand party of yours."

Jilly didn't answer when Katrina rang her number that evening. In a way Katrina was glad. She knew she'd tell Jilly about Larry sometime, but just now she didn't feel like discussing him. Somehow, to have him spoken about in Jilly's frivolous fashion would have seemed almost sacrilegious, and she went to bed early so she could go over in her mind every detail of her time spent at River Cottage with Larry.

Already it seemed ages since his departure; she felt desolate without him, and twisting round on the pillows, she pushed her fist against her mouth. She had to stop thinking about him like this or she would end up not only with a bruised heart, but a broken one. If his feelings for her had been in any way serious he would have promised to ring her, or at least have given her a number to contact, but he had done neither. The things he'd said to her yesterday on the moors meant nothing after all.

She lay sleepless into the small hours of morning, her thoughts going round in circles. Eventually she made herself a vow: from now on she was going to fill every one of her waking hours usefully and pleasantly. The end of her holiday would come soon enough and there was no sense wasting what was left of it in useless dreams.

Chapter Seventeen

OVER the next two days Katrina did all the things she'd promised herself at the start of the holiday. She went for solitary walks by winding rivers and trudged over the moors to the lower hill slopes. She'd learned to ride as a child and now rose early to go hacking over frost-rimmed fields on the broad back of Clover, a dapple-grey mare with a sweet temperament, and an endearing habit of trotting home unguided to her stable.

Belle kept Clover at the farm out of the goodness of her heart. A friend in Aberdeen ran a riding stables and when Clover reached retirement age she'd been earmarked for the knacker's yard till Belle intervened and offered to let the horse spend the rest of her days at Balgower.

Katrina was finding out more and more about the Grants as the days went by. If they could do anyone a good turn, they did so willingly and without fuss. In his way, Bob was just as soft-hearted as his wife and had seldom grumbled at the amount of lame dogs which found their way to the farm at some point or other. Everyone in the community liked and respected them and Katrina found herself growing ever closer to them. She felt completely at home in their company; they let her come and go as she pleased and made her feel as if she was very much a part of the family.

Having Belle as a companion was a refreshing and often hilarious experience, and when she announced one morning she would like to go to Aviemore to do her Christmas shopping, Katrina said she'd accompany her.

"I'll just give Aunt Annie a ring first," Belle decided.

"Aunt Annie?" Katrina asked.

"You don't mind, do you, dear?" Belle was already half-way up the hall, "I said I would let her know when I was doing the shopping. She has some bits and bobs she wants to get for the family. Mind you, it won't be much; she breeds moths in her purse, but a change of scene will do her good and she'll enjoy seeing you again."

Aunt Annie's family: a son and a daughter, both married with five children between them, lived in Aberdeen and England respectively. Aunt Annie didn't see all that much of them, but they'd been concerned enough about her welfare to coax her to have a phone installed at her croft. The instrument did not meet with her approval. It made funny noises, she said. She was certain other phone users could tap into her line and listen to her business; sometimes it rang and there was nobody there, and she was highly suspicious of wrong-number callers – claiming they were only ringing to see if she was out so they could descend and rob her home of its valuables.

Despite all that, it was difficult to get her off the phone once she got warmed up, and on this occasion she spoke to Belle for fully fifteen minutes, during which time she complained about everything and said it was a bit much to expect her to get ready for town at such short notice. In the end, however, she graciously consented to make herself presentable for the trip and hung up with a horse-like snort because the postman was at the door, as if she wasn't harassed enough already.

Bob ran Katrina and Belle to River Cottage to collect the Mini, now completely free of snow. Katrina hardly dared look at the sturdy white cottage against the hills, and something tugged at her heart as she spied a shapeless mound of snow near the door – the remains of the snowman. A bittersweet yearning flooded her being and she was forced to face the fact that she was missing Larry more than she could have believed possible.

Aunt Annie soon took everyone's minds off anything else, however. When she heard the car stopping she came out of the crofthouse, dressed from head to foot in heather coloured tweed, a large modern duffel bag that her daughter had given her swinging cheekily from one stooped shoulder, the grouse feather in her hat prodding boldly skywards in brave defiance of the wind which was whistling in over the loch.

"Well, I made it, despite everything," she greeted Belle sourly. "That postman! He always comes at the most awkward moments, and he expects tea every time. Where he puts it all, I don't know, and I daren't ask in case he tells me in detail. All I can say is, it's a good job there are plenty of bushes growing along his route. Rain or shine, Joe will water them – otherwise he'd burst!" She spotted Katrina sitting in the car and her face broke into a smile. "It's yourself, lass, move over and we'll have a good blether on the way to town. I enjoyed your visit when you came to see me that last time. It did my heart

159

good to have somebody young about the place." It was no easy matter getting Aunt Annie and her feather into the Mini in one piece, but at last they were all settled and soon pottering around the Aviemore shops.

Belle had been right about Aunt Annie; she never opened her purse if she could at all help it. When she heard the prices of goods on display, she hummed and hawed and kept her companions thoroughly occupied as they tried to advise her on what to buy.

"Och, go away and leave me be," she said eventually. "I'll be far better looking at things on my own, and you two no doubt want to get on with your own shopping. I'll meet you back here in an hour, when surely we'll all have found what we want." At that she gave Katrina a conspiratorial wink. "Buy Larry something nice, he's a good lad, and though he'll likely have everything already there's bound to be something he'd appreciate."

"Oh, but—"

"Oh, but, nothing. I know all about you and him. Joe the Post has a big mouth. He's heard a few snippets on his visits to Balgower and managed to put a few of them together. Don't worry, none of it amounts to much, but unlike him I can tell you're in love. I might be an old wife, but I can still remember what it was like when I had my Jeemie."

"Aunt Annie," Katrina laughed. "You're a rogue but I love you for it."

Belle had wandered off. Katrina took stock of her surroundings before heading up the road to visit one or two gift shops where she bought presents for Belle and Bob and other local people she knew. After that she crossed the road and went into the jewellers. The man behind the counter was very helpful, and when Katrina didn't seem too sure of what she wanted, he brought out trays of watches and cufflinks for her to look at.

"No," she shook her head.

"How about one of these, then?" He pointed to a case. Her face lit, and there and then she purchased a sterling silver identity bracelet with gold finished links. She left it behind so Larry's name could be engraved on it and came out of the shop flushed and full of doubts. He would possibly see such a gift as a sign that he meant more to her than just a casual lover, and he mightn't welcome the idea.

On the pavement outside she bumped into Belle, who laid her doubts to rest by voicing her enthusiastic approval. Nevertheless, to compensate for her rash decision, Katrina went into a stationers and bought several packets of pencils and some notebooks in the hope that Larry would view the whole thing in a lighthearted fashion.

Yet, at the same time she realised the solace she had come to Scotland to find now seemed impossibly out of reach. A restlessness surged in her veins and while she longed for Larry even now, she blamed him for disrupting her future plans. If he hadn't intruded she would have gone back refreshed to London to resume her old job and pick up the threads of her life with enthusiasm, instead of which she was unable to look forward to any kind of future which didn't include him.

Her thoughts were dismal at this point, but Aunt Annie came to the rescue once again. She was waiting at the appointed place as she'd said, and to the complete astonishment of her companions, she whisked them off to lunch in a nearby hotel, no expense spared.

"I've enjoyed myself today," she said jubilantly as she unhooked her duffel bag and sat back in her seat. "It isn't often I get the chance to eat out, so let's have a ball! On me! A whole three courser, and maybe some wine to pep us up?"

"I'm driving," Belle reminded her.

"*I'm* not!" Aunt Annie was being positively abandoned. "You can drink orange juice. Me and Katrina will get a half-bottle of Hock between us and to hell with poverty!"

The waitress came up to take their order. Aunt Annie leaned forward to look at the menu, her feather tickling the girl's face as she bent with her pencil poised above her notepad. Belle and Katrina giggled, Aunt Annie snorted, and the waitress gave an uncertain smile before she too joined in the merriment.

Chapter Eighteen

IT was early afternoon when Belle and Katrina got home and they had no sooner shut the door behind them when the phone went. It was Jilly, sounding slightly miffed that Katrina hadn't been in touch, but reverting back to her cheerful self when Katrina explained to her she'd been out when she had last tried to return the call.

"Oh, well, I've got you now, I expect we've both been busy. I'm phoning from the office, just a quickie on the off chance I'd get you in. Last time we spoke I thought you sounded different and I still think it. You *do* sound different. Sort of pent up, if you know what I mean. Don't tell me you've bagged a Highland laird *already*?"

"Hardly that," said Katrina dryly.

"But there *is* a man?" persisted Jilly.

"Y-yes," Katrina admitted. The urge to talk about Larry was still strong in her heart. "A novelist called Larry Sinclair. According to Belle he's well known, though my knowledge of that side of him only consists of what I've heard. He was born and brought up here and comes back to write his books."

"Larry Sinclair—" There was a long pause.

"Are you still there, Jilly?" asked Katrina.

"Yes, I'm still here."

"What's wrong? Have you heard of him?"

Jilly's laugh sounded forced. "Who hasn't? His novels aren't the only things to give him a reputation in these parts. He's made it with more girls than you've had hot dinners!" she laughed again. "He even made it to the gossip columns. You must be blind as well as deaf."

"I don't read the gossip columns," Katrina said coldly, though her mouth had gone dry. "They're full of banal rubbish. Who's to say they're accurate?"

"I can vouch for it." Jilly sounded smug. "As far as Larry's concerned, anyway."

"You know him then – personally?" Katrina remembered Larry's reaction on hearing Jilly's name.

"A friend of mine is an editor at his publishers and she invited me to an author's do. Larry was there—" she released her breath in a whoosh. "What a guy! He's a quick worker. The fastest draw I've ever met. He aims for the jackpot every time."

Katrina put a hand on the table to steady herself. "Jilly – you mean . . . ?"

Jilly's voice came incredulously over the line. "Aw, c'mon, Katie, don't be so *naïve*. This *is* the twentieth century! Girls no longer wear chastity belts." Katrina couldn't speak and Jilly said sharply, "Katie, don't tell me you've been taken in by him? Oh, God, I'm sorry, but believe me he isn't for you. Don't forget, you already made a mistake with a guy like him. Only one difference, Larry's a *real* sex bomb! He knows how to turn a girl on."

Katrina felt so sick she barely managed to mutter, "I'll-I'll have to go. I want to phone Peggy."

"Oh – how is the dear old mother hen?"

"If you mean Peggy, I won't know until I've spoken to her. Bye, Jilly, if I don't manage to get in touch over Christmas, have a nice time."

"Don't worry, I will. At least, I think so; there isn't so much going on in the way of parties as I thought – and I miss you about the place, Katie."

Katrina carefully returned the receiver in its cradle. There was a numbness in the pit of her stomach and she shook her head as if to clear it.

Belle came into the room, halting at sight of Katrina's face. "What has that friend of yours been saying, Katrina? You look upset."

"Oh, it's nothing, Belle, she's just missing me, that's all. I was wondering, I know I'm running up the bill, but could I please give Peggy Melville a quick call? You know, the girl I told you about, the one who married a doctor?"

"Of course you can, Katrina," Belle said warmly and went out of the room, shutting the door discreetly behind her.

Katrina rang the number in Inverness. Peggy was delighted to hear from her and after a few pleasantries suggested that Katrina spend the night with her. "Peter's away at a medical conference and won't be back till tomorrow," Peggy explained in her unhurried fashion, making no attempt to quell the persistent demands of her small daughter who was trying to wrest the phone from her hands. "If you stay till tomorrow, at least it will give us time for a good old natter. Hang on and I'll tell you how to get here." They spoke for a few minutes more, then there was a pause; Peggy had obviously turned her attention elsewhere. When she came back on the line she said somewhat breathlessly, "I must go, Fiona needs changing and Jamie's screaming to be fed. Look forward to meeting you."

Katrina sought out Belle and outlined her plans, rather apologetically explaining that she would need the Mini once more. Belle was not perturbed. "Just be back in time for Christmas, that's all I ask. You'd best leave me your address and phone number in case I need to be in touch."

"I'll only be gone for one night," Katrina laughed and went upstairs to pack a few things.

She was quite used now to the temperamental habits of Belle's little car and made good time to Inverness, though once there she had difficulty following Peggy's rather scrappy directions. She felt she must have scoured every street in the neat housing estate before she finally unearthed Peggy's terrace house, situated at the top of an oval. Peggy was genuinely pleased to see her and made a determined effort to clear a passage through the jumble of toys in the hall.

"It's been so *long*, Katie," she grinned, tucking a wilful strand of baby-fine hair behind her ear, and leading the way into a pleasant, airy room with lemon walls and cream-coloured wool easy chairs which looked rather the worse for wear. It was a family room however, with a cosy, friendly atmosphere and Katrina voiced her admiration warmly.

Peggy looked around her and shrugged. "Peter was right when he said light furniture would be a disaster," she grinned ruefully. "Next time everything, except the walls, will be darker than dark. It won't be in this house, though. Peter's doing so well we've decided to move to the country, into a nice old-fashioned house where the children will have room to grow up." She gazed thoughtfully at a chewed model of Paddington Bear and seemed lost in contemplation of the furry toy. A rangy, big-boned girl, dressed casually in jeans and a baggy sweater, she would have been plain but for her large, expressive grey eyes and a devastatingly sweet smile.

Hugging Paddington to her bosom she sat down on the couch and patted the space at her side. "Sit down and give me all your news. Fiona's having a nap and Jamie's been fed, so we should have peace for a while." But it wasn't till after dinner, when Katrina had helped bathe the children and put them to bed, that there was really time to talk. Both girls flopped down on the couch and grinned at each other. Nappies and baby clothes littered the chairs; Jamie's bath was still on its stand by the fire, but with a careless flip of her hand Peggy motioned that tidying up could wait till later.

Katrina went through to the kitchen and somehow found a jar of coffee which she made and carried into the sitting room. Peggy took the mug gratefully and, easing her shoes from her feet, sat back, curling her toes into the rug. "*Now*, give me *all* the news," she instructed. "Every little thing that's happened since I saw you last."

Katrina explained about her mother, then found herself pouring out everything about Larry. From being unwilling to mention his name, she now wanted to talk and talk about him, as if by doing so she could bring him a step nearer, oust him out of the confines of her heart where fiercely conflicting emotions seemed to be getting her nowhere at all.

"A writer?" Peggy exclaimed in delight. "Not *the* Larry Sinclair? Gosh—" she sat back, her eyes big with awe. "Peter is an avid fan. He's got all the Larry Sinclair books in the bedroom." Her wide mouth stretched into a maternally indulgent grin. "It's one of the few places still safe from Fiona's little fingers. She's into everything at the moment." She considered her friend with unusual seriousness. "You've got it bad, haven't you, Katie?"

Katrina played with the chain at her neck. "I-I don't really know how I feel. Mixed up, I suppose. Anyway, he's not the type to take any woman seriously, so what's the use of speculating?"

"How do you know?" asked Peggy frankly.

"I – well, I hardly know him . . . except – I-I gather he's had a few affairs. He more or less told me himself he's had quite a lot of experience with women."

"You know him well enough to blush every time you mention his name. Anyway, the length of time you know a man isn't important. It's how you feel that matters. Look at me and Peter—" she laughed infectiously. "He literally bowled me over from the start and it's worked for us. The Lord knows he puts up with a lot from me – well, I'm hardly the perfect housewife – but somehow, that doesn't seem to matter. We overlook each other's faults and see the good points. I mean, look at you and Paul; that didn't work out yet you had bags of time to get to know one another – only he was smart enough, or cunning enough, to fool you for quite some time. At least Larry hasn't tried to deceive you into thinking he's a little goody-goody. He's been honest with you, and for that you should be thankful."

Katrina was somewhat taken aback at Peggy's

response. She had glimpsed this serious side occasionally in the past, but it appeared that marriage had strengthened her friend's hitherto rather scatterbrained ideas. To cover her surprise she said laughingly, "Jilly wouldn't let affairs of the heart get her down. It's all like water off a duck's back where she's concerned. She's only out for a good time and somehow manages to get it without becoming too involved."

A frown marred Peggy's sweet face. "Jilly's a high flier. She only gives the impression of being frivolous. All those male acquaintances of hers are only a cover. She's a professional gold-digger – when she makes a landing it'll be a big one and then she'll dispense with the fry without batting an eyelid."

"That's putting it a bit harshly," Katrina said defensively. "You never really liked Jilly, did you?"

Peggy made a face. "She always poked fun at me behind my back. She couldn't understand how an ugly duckling like me managed to bag a man like Peter—" She held up her hand as Katrina opened her mouth to make a conciliatory comment. "Katie, give me some credit. Jilly just tolerated me, and to be honest I only tolerated her because I knew you and she were such good friends. I didn't want to lose you, so I strung along and said nothing."

Katrina, remembering some of Jilly's derogatory comments about Peggy, felt uncomfortable. Nevertheless she was moved to protest. "Jilly's not really like that. She is a bit giddy, I admit, and tends to say things she doesn't mean . . ."

"Not giddy – the very opposite," said Peggy, her brow creased. "Have you told her about Larry?"

"Yes, this afternoon, just before I rang you."

Peggy looked at her friend's face and her lips tightened. "What *exactly* did she say to you, Katie? You look upset at the very thought of it."

"That's the understatement of the year! Let's just say I've been – enlightened."

"What about?"

"Larry. Jilly knows him – rather well – and so it seems does half of London."

Peggy tutted angrily. "Katie . . . You mustn't take as gospel everything Jilly tells you."

Katrina pressed her cold palms together. "She just confirmed what I already suspected. Hearing it put into words just brought it fully home. I – there isn't any more to say on the subject. I don't want to see Larry again."

"But there *is* more to say, *lots* more," Peggy said insistently. "At least give yourself a chance to get to know him better. You're not being fair – to him or yourself."

Katrina passed a hand wearily over her eyes. "No, Peggy, I don't intend to become another of his conquests . . ." her lips twisted and she added bitterly, "What am I saying? It's already too late, I've allowed myself to become just that. Oh, hell! This is the last thing I wanted to happen! Why can't I just have lighthearted affairs like everyone else?"

"Sleep on it," advised Peggy gently. "Your room's ready. I've put the blanket on at two, so you'll be nice and snug."

"Thanks, Peggy, I will. I'll say goodnight now. Don't worry about me, I'll be perfectly all right, and I didn't come here to burden you with my woes."

Peggy put a hand on her shoulder and squeezed it. "That's what friends are for, Katie, to share the good as well as the bad."

Katrina hugged her friend and went out of the room. The little guest bedroom that Peggy had shown her earlier was neat and tidy, and was such a complete contrast to the rest of the house Katrina guessed it was the only room out of bounds to little Fiona. If she hadn't been so tense, she would have found the warm pink of the decor relaxing. As it was, when she climbed into the comfortable single bed she tossed and turned, unable to sleep, going over and over in her mind the things that Jilly had told her.

It was almost four when she finally drifted into a fitful slumber, broken by images of Larry's handsome face and her own cries of helplessness deep inside her head.

Chapter Nineteen

KATRINA awoke with a start, hot and uncomfortable, little beads of perspiration moistening her face and neck. A thin, wailing sound reached her. For a few moments she was disorientated, then realised she was hearing Jamie crying from a room along the hall.

Sleep fled and in its place grew a dull, sick ache of misery. Bottles clinked. It was still dark but the milkman was coming up the garden path and she decided to get up and make Peggy a cup of tea. The house was cold; she washed quickly and hastily pulled on a pair of jeans and a cosy mohair sweater.

Peggy was in the kitchen, wrapped in a tartan wool dressing gown, yawning wearily as she bounced Jamie on one arm and with her free hand, prepared his feed. Her grey eyes opened in surprise at the sight of Katrina and, between yawns, told her that she needn't have got up. "You'll have to make allowances for me," she said in a slurred voice. "I limit myself to grunts at this unearthly hour. Peter swears that Jamie's first intelligible sounds will consist of a series of yawning snorts."

Katrina smiled affectionately into her friend's pale face and went to put on the kettle. Her own thoughts were fragmentary and made little sense. All she knew with certainty was that she had no intention of seeing Larry again and she bitterly regretted having encouraged him to come back to Scotland for Christmas. She voiced her thoughts to Peggy an hour later when they had put Jamie back to bed and were seated with second mugs of tea by the comforting heat of the gas fire in the sitting room.

"Don't be silly, Katie," was Peggy's rather tight-lipped reply. "Of course you'll have to see him again, be it sooner or later. Larry comes here to write his books and your relatives will expect you back for holidays so, whatever you intend doing now, you're bound to meet up again."

"That doesn't mean I have to speak to him."

Peggy pushed her hair behind her ears. "Meantime, you're going to let him come all the way back here, only to give him the cold shoulder?"

Katrina shook her head vehemently. "No – not if I can help it. I don't have his home number, but I might get it if I phone his publisher."

"They won't give it to you," Peggy pointed out bluntly. "I know someone who tried to winkle a favourite author's address out of a publisher only to be refused, politely but firmly. Besides, they'll most likely be shut up for Christmas – it's only three days away, remember."

"I'll have to try," Katrina meant to sound firm but there was a quaver in her voice and when she picked up the phone later to get the publisher's number from directory enquiries, she wasn't sure in her mind just what she would say, should she get a reply. But Peggy had been right, there was no answer from the publisher's office, and in desperation Katrina depressed the button and dialled Belle's number.

Belle was pleased to hear Katrina's voice and a few words passed between them before Katrina said urgently, "Belle, listen, I'm-I'm staying with Peggy for another night . . ." She glanced at her friend in silent pleading for confirmation and Peggy slowly nodded her agreement. "If Larry comes looking for me, don't tell him where I am—" Belle's protesting questions floated down the line but Katrina stemmed them rather abruptly and put the phone down to look shamefaced at Peggy. "I'm sorry I sprung that on you, Peggy – do you mind?"

"Of course not. Peter won't get back till tonight and I love having your company, only – Katie, it isn't like you to take this way out."

Katrina pressed her fingers to her temples. "Try to understand, Peggy," she said, and there was a note of despair in her voice, "If I see him again, I don't think I'll be strong enough to withstand him, and I must – I *must* – before it's too late."

"Isn't it already?" was Peggy's only comment before she went to rescue the toys Fiona had thrown from her playpen.

Katrina's nerves stretched tighter as the morning wore on. It was quite possible that Larry might return today and she was struck by the thought that he could at any minute be arriving at Dalcross Airport, just a mile or so from Peggy's house.

All sorts of wild ideas went through her head. She thought of phoning the airport for arrival times and then going to apprehend him, with the intention of telling him, face to face, that his journey had been wasted. She tortured herself with several variations on the same theme, but in the end came back to one hard fact: if she set eyes on him again she would weaken, and all her resolutions would melt like snow under a tropical sun. For Peggy's sake she managed to maintain a cheerful front but when, just after lunch, the phone shrilled out, she jumped violently and turned away while Peggy went to answer it.

"It's for you," Peggy held out the handset. "Belle," she added, at her friend's gaze of inquiry.

"Katrina," Belle's tones were firm and brooked no nonsense. "Larry's home, he got in this morning and phoned a short time ago asking to speak to you."

"What – what did you tell him?"

"I said you were visiting a friend or rather, staying with one. He asked me where and I told him I wasn't sure of the address and that I had mislaid the phone number. He asked me to look for it and said he would phone back in a couple of hours . . ."

"Belle, you mustn't tell him where I am – *please* – I-I need time to think."

"Katrina, you'll have to come back sometime and you'll see him anyway, so why put it off?"

"He – might not stay," Katrina said weakly.

"On the other hand, he might be waiting to wring your neck when you finally decide to turn up," Belle sounded unusually angry. "Why don't you phone him and tell him you're finished with him? It would be fair to put him in the picture right away."

Katrina drew a deep breath. "Yes, Belle, I had thought of that, but – oh God! I'm sorry. I'm just rather mixed up at the moment." Katrina, on the verge of tears, was both angry and surprised at herself. She had never felt so utterly miserable before – the heartache she had endured over Paul was nothing compared with this.

"You must do as you think best," Belle's voice was kinder now. "Naturally I'm disappointed, and to be honest I'm as curious as hell to know the reasons behind it all but, whatever happens, I'll expect you back here for Christmas. You might need a shoulder by then and I'm always here if you need me."

Peggy had been hovering nearby and as soon as Katrina put the phone down she said pleasantly, "Well, *are* you?"

"Am I what?" Katrina asked dazedly.

"Going to phone Larry?"

Katrina nodded, "Yes – yes I am." Before she could change her mind she dialled the number for River Cottage, her tongue circling dry lips as she waited in anticipatory suspense for Larry's voice to come over the line. But there was no answer. She let the number ring for a full minute, just in case he might be outside chopping logs or doing any of a number of things she had come to associate with his routine at the cottage. Her hand flew to her mouth as vivid pictures flashed through her mind, how she had loved it all: the river, the moors, the house, the den with its fire leaping in the grate, she and Larry chatting so easily together – the rapture she had known with him there.

No other woman had shared the cottage with him before, of that she was almost certain. There had been no feminine traces, only manly touches; a man who loved books, who treasured family heirlooms, who loved pictures of wild animals and of the sea, who was definitely untidy in his own little domain but who was scrupulously attentive when it came to other matters. And he was also accomplished in the kitchen, taking quite a pride in his culinary efforts, yet in no way did this detract from his charisma . . .

Katrina banged the phone down, aware of a terrible sensation of anti-climax in the pit of her stomach.

Peggy was cradling Jamie in her arms over by the fire. "Katie, I know how you feel," she said kindly. "Well, perhaps I don't, not really. Until Peter came along there was nobody – nobody worth mentioning that is – and I was lucky enough to get the man I wanted without any hitches. Peter was so busy making his way as a doctor he didn't have the time for girls, so there wasn't a lot in his past for me to get het up about . . ." She looked thoughtful as she continued, "Larry's a different kettle of fish. He's led a rather glamorous life to date – at least, that's the impression one gets. His picture is on the cover of his books and he's really gorgeous – the kind of man women would fight tooth and nail over. Yet, have you ever thought – a man like that might never have any true feelings for women who are—"

"*Easy,*" interrupted Katrina, saying the word scathingly. "Peggy, *I'm* in that category now. I've been to bed with him for heaven's sake! And while I wasn't exactly a pushover, I did give in. In the end I capitulated like – like all the others, and in his eyes I'm just like them now."

Peggy's sweet face was full of sympathy as she noticed how white and strained Katrina looked. "You're welcome to stay here as long as you like – you know that, Katie. You were the only girl I ever really confided in and when I needed advice you always gave it willingly." She sighed. "That's why I hate seeing you going to pieces like this. It's so unlike the Katie I know and if Larry affects you that badly it's perhaps as well you've decided to finish it between you – though I still think you ought to give the whole thing a chance to get off the ground." She cuddled Jamie and kissed his smooth little cheek. "Larry aside, you can't let your relatives down, though. Belle's arranging a party for you and you'll have to go back for that at least."

"I know! I *know!*" cried Katrina distractedly, pushing aside a desperate urge to pack her case and get back to London as quickly as she could.

Chapter Twenty

TWICE in the course of the afternoon Katrina tried Larry's number, but each time there was no reply and she was trying to decide what to do next when the matter was taken out of her hands. Standing in the bay window with Jamie in her arms, she saw his red MG sliding to a halt beside the Mini. Horrified, she watched as Larry unfolded himself from the driving seat, banging the door forcibly behind him. He stood for a long moment, scanning the windows with calculated deliberation, and Katrina, her heart palpitating madly, stepped back a few paces.

He came up the path, something menacing about the way he covered the ground with such effortless ease. Katrina didn't know whether to turn and run to her room or stay and face him as bravely as she could. The doorbell shrilled and she found she was rooted to the spot, quite unable to go and answer it. She heard Peggy's steps in the hall, followed by the low murmur of voices, and when Larry was shown into the room she remained like a statue at the window, only dimly aware of Peggy plucking Jamie from her arms.

"Stay, Peggy, please," her lips felt numb and her voice sounded strangely shrill to her own ears. "You don't have to leave your own sitting room." But Peggy murmured something about rousing Fiona from her nap and went out of the room.

Larry stood just inside the doorway. If it hadn't been for the oddly dark colour of his eyes in an otherwise expressionless face, she could almost have believed his frame of mind was as relaxed as his appearance. He had reverted back to casual clothes and she half-fooled herself that the encounter wasn't going to be nearly as dreadful as she imagined. But his voice when he spoke slashed over her like barbs of steel. "Just what the hell do you think you're playing at?" he demanded and she noticed the slow clenching of fists at his sides.

She braced herself, unconsciously tilting her chin in a gesture of defiance. "I'm – I'm not playing at anything."

"Oh, aren't you?" There were undertones of mockery in the words. "I should have thought you were playing a very childish game, and if not, can you explain why you instructed Belle not to let on where you were?"

"She – oh, why did she tell you?" she protested on a half sob.

His lips twisted contemptuously. "Belle's a sensible woman, Katie. Perhaps she didn't want to be a partner in your nasty little prank." He took a step forward and as panic choked her she looked over her shoulder as if seeking a way of escape.

She twisted her fingers together nervously. "Please, Larry, leave me alone. Since you went away I've had time to think and I've come to the decision that it would be best for both of us if we didn't see each other again . . ."

"Since when did you make my decisions for me? What's

best for you doesn't necessarily apply to me." The words were heavy with sarcasm.

"I-I tried to phone you," she persisted, "but there was no answer, either from your publishers or from you at the cottage. I'm sorry you've had such a wasted journey."

His face blazed into fury. "*Sorry!* And so you bloody well should be! I almost broke my neck getting back north to see you. I'm damned if I'm leaving here without some answers and they had better be good because the way I'm feeling right now it would give me the greatest pleasure to break your bloody neck!"

Katrina's face drained of colour. She looked so vulnerable with her chestnut hair emphasising the pallor of her skin. Her mohair sweater looked too big on such small shoulders, and if he hadn't been so incensed his instinct would have been to take her in his arms and kiss her in the way he'd imagined a thousand times since leaving her.

He had cut short several commitments in order to be with her the sooner, and – stupid bastard that he was! – he had honestly expected she would be pleased to see him again. Instead of which . . . His jaw clenched and he said tersely, "Well?"

Helplessly she shook her head. "Larry, please try to understand, I'm just not ready for – for the sort of affair you have in mind—"

"It's Carrington, isn't it?" he asked harshly. "You've already made up your mind that this thing we have will end up as disastrously as your lousy affair with him. Is that it, Katie?"

"I-I don't know what to think. I can't see into the future, but I know this. I don't intend to get hurt again and that's final. I'll admit that what we had was good but the fact that I went to bed with you doesn't mean—"

"*Good!*" he interposed incredulously, "Is that the best you can do? Why the hell can't you admit there was more to it than just two people hopping into bed together. You became alive, Katie, I could see and feel it happening to you. What's the point in denying it – that and the fact you wanted me every bit as much as I wanted you? Am I wrong? I really would like to know."

Katrina felt so weak she thought she was going to faint, and she caught at a chair for support. She was on the point of blurting out everything Jilly had told her, but in his present mood she doubted if he would understand she just wasn't like the other women he'd known. It would sound silly and trite. He moved in a different world from hers and might not be able to accept her way of thinking. "Larry," she whispered, "what do you want me to say? That I'm grateful to you for—"

Two long strides carried him over the room and his hands shot out to grip her shoulders so painfully she winced. "Don't be such a damned fool! It doesn't suit you!" he punched the words at her savagely. "And I don't take kindly to being insulted by anyone – let alone you, Katie." Katrina tilted her head further back in an effort to escape his wrath. He looked down at her; her shoulders felt fragile under his bruising grip and he relaxed it slightly. "Katie," he said unsteadily. "Why are we fighting like this? Why?"

Lost for words she merely shook her head.

"Katie," the deep tones of his voice were laden with intimacy, but she knew she couldn't let that voice, those hands, sway her from the path she had set herself.

"Katie," he said again, "Don't you see we were meant to meet one another? We can't rub out what has happened – we can't stop the things that are meant for us."

The words were a soft caress in her ears, his head was blotting out the light, his lips brushing the warm hollow of her throat. "You – mustn't." The protest was only a gesture. It meant nothing and he knew it. With a soft sigh of resignation she melted against him and gave herself up to his kisses . . .

A baby's cry echoed down the hall. "Peggy," Katrina said unsteadily, "she – might come in."

He let her go abruptly and raked the hair away from his brow. Katrina turned away from him as she said, "Larry, this doesn't mean anything has changed, and – please believe me when I say you are the last person in the world I would wish to insult. You awakened me, I'll give you that . . . But – it was no new experience for you – you must admit that."

His hand shot out once more to pull her round to face him, and his eyes were blue ice chips in his blazing face. "So, that's it?" he ground out through clenched teeth. "The same old theme. Because I've enjoyed having women in my life you imagine you're just going to become another conquest, to be used then forgotten. Well, let me tell you something, the only reason I invited you into a domain that no other woman has ever entered was because you are not *like* any woman I've ever met.

"I knew from the start that as far as I was concerned, you were, for want of a better word, different. Sometimes there's a special chemistry between a man and a woman. We had it, Katie, and it wasn't just good. It was

185

wonderful. I glimpsed something in you, a rare thing that set you apart – now I'm rapidly changing my mind. You're different all right – you're bloody impossible!"

She tore herself free of his grasp and retreated backwards. "Then, in that case, it might be wise if-if you don't try to see me again."

"Too bloody right I won't!" he slashed at her. "Next time I need a woman I'll go for the human variety – not a robot who can turn herself off at the press of a button! My apologies to your friend for barging into her house like this. Too bad she had to be involved." He strode out to the hall, banging the outside door behind him. Through a misty blur Katrina saw him take the steps down to the path three at a time.

The next moment Peggy was outside in the hall, the front door was opened once more and Katrina heard her calling, "Mr Sinclair, please wait!" Katrina watched as Peggy flew down the path and apprehended Larry at the gate. He paused and swiftly wrote something in the book she'd proffered. A few words were exchanged before he went through the gate and climbed into the MG. Katrina turned blindly and collapsed into a nearby chair. The roar of the powerful engine, familiar to her now, filled her eardrums and seemed to reverberate through the house.

Peggy came back, hugging one of Larry's books to her chest, unable to keep the triumph out of her grey eyes. "Peter will be thrilled," she said breathlessly. "I mean, it isn't every day a famous author visits your house. I can't believe I was able to get his signature first hand." With shining face she thumbed through the book and the back cover fell open. Katrina bit her lip as Larry's face leapt out at her. Peggy drew back. "I'm a fool, Katie. I'm always putting my foot in it. I-I couldn't help hearing you and Larry sort of – well – having words, and yet here I am rattling on about a silly autograph." She inclined her head. "Do you think he'll go back to London?"

"I expect so – he certainly won't have any desire to see me again, not after me telling him we were more or less finished."

"Did you tell him why?"

"No, I couldn't. I couldn't seem to think of the right words, but I think he guessed anyway."

Peggy sighed. "It all seems rather unbalanced somehow. I mean, he *did* have a right to know why you gave him the brush off. I realise I didn't meet him at a very suitable time, but he seems so nice and so much more good-looking than his photo. You and he would have made such an attractive couple."

Katrina got up to throw her arm over Peggy's shoulder. "C'mon, Pegs, this isn't your worry. You must be heartily sick of all this drama on your front doorstep, so to speak. Look, let's wrap the children up and get out of the house for a while. I have some last minute shopping to do, so we'll just pile into the Mini and pray it stays in one piece."

Peggy's face cleared. "Right," she said gaily. "We'll take the baby buggy with us and pop the pair of them into it later. And we might just splash out on fish suppers to bring home with us. On second thoughts, Peter will be back sometime this evening. I'd better make him something decent, though I've seen us both tucking into fish and chips and not

187

even using plates – he says they taste better out of paper."

"We'll cook up something between us," Katrina promised, and went to help Peggy get the children ready, all the while trying to pretend to herself she had done the right thing sending Larry away, even though she was already bitterly regretting it.

Walking round the Inverness shops with Peggy and the children, she began to cheer up. It was difficult to remain in the doldrums in Peggy's company. The stores were bright with festive lights and gifts, and she was delighted with all she saw, exclaiming over everything, chattering away in her abandoned manner.

It was a dry day and so mild that Katrina commented on it to Peggy, who nodded and smiled. "The weather's a great topic in this part of the world. You can have four seasons in a day – I've seen hail in the morning, rain in the afternoon, mist at teatime, and the sun blinking out just before it goes down. Everybody moans about it, it's the done thing; but when the sun really does shine, it's the loveliest place to be and I really enjoy living here."

When they finished shopping they didn't go straight home, but went to visit one of Peggy's neighbours in the oval; a round young woman with straight brown hair, a cheery smile and a straightforward manner. She was also the mother of a very lively toddler and the visitors were no sooner over the threshold than she popped Peggy's two into a large playpen in the corner beside her own, gave them each a tube of chocolate buttons, and said briskly, "There, that should keep them quiet for a while. They'll make a helluva mess, but soap and water will soon sort that out."

Peggy introduced Katrina to her friend. "And this is Penny Martin," she went on. "She and I are known in these parts as the terrible two. I can't think why," she gave a merry laugh. "All we do is talk and swap recipes and look after each other's kids."

"I can think of a thousand reasons!" Penny ran her hand through her hair, leaving it standing on end. "I'll go and make some coffee and then we'll have a gossip. There's always plenty going on in the oval; it's like a goldfish bowl, but Lord knows what I'd do if I couldn't see what other people are up to. Jim, that's my husband, calls me a rubber neck, but hell! Where's the harm? We all watch one another and thoroughly enjoy it, and if anyone's in trouble there's always someone to lend a helping hand."

It was a totally entertaining experience being in the company of Peggy and Penny. They vied with one another as to who could say the most in the shortest possible time; they laughed and exchanged small snippets about the progress of their children, bringing Katrina into their conversation with ease, even though, as Penny said, she had still to find out the joys and tribulations of motherhood.

The talk swung round to men and Penny wasted no time in sentiment when she said bluntly to Katrina, "What about you, Katie? Do you have one? A man, I mean? Or should that be in the plural?"

"No to all three," Katrina said lightly. "I came north for a holiday and that's what I intend to have."

"I don't believe it," Penny stated with unnerving frankness.

"And neither should you," Peggy glanced apologetically at Katrina as she spoke, but went on determinedly, "She's been seeing Larry Sinclair. He came to my house this very day and signed a book for Peter."

"*Larry Sinclair!*" For once Penny was lost for words but soon recovered her powers of speech. "Gosh and double gosh! Jim isn't much of a reader but he *has* read Larry Sinclair. Really, Peggy—" she rounded on her friend, "you might have brought him over, just for a minute to let me touch him. I saw him once on telly and nearly broke the set to get at him." She swung back to Katrina. "Come on then, Katie, tell us what it's like to be in close contact with a hunk like that."

"It was good while it lasted," Katrina tried to be flippant, "which wasn't for very long. We split, it was the best thing for us both."

"You mean to say you let him go?" Penny's eyes were round. Sitting back she fanned herself and stared at her visitor in disbelief, and it was as well for Katrina that the children began clamouring for attention so insistently they succeeded in taking it away from herself.

She was glad when, shortly afterwards, Peggy decided to make a move, and they all left; Penny's enthusiastic invitation to come back soon ringing in their ears.

Peter came home that evening to a great welcome from his wife and children. He was a tall, thin young man with cropped fair hair, glasses, and a rather serious mouth. Katrina soon discovered however, that his looks belied his nature. He and Peggy were a perfect match for one another; they laughed at little things, gazed at one another affectionately, argued good-naturedly about small domestic matters, and caught each other's hands whenever opportunity presented itself.

When the children had been bathed and put to bed, dinner was served by Peggy in a rather haphazard fashion through the hatch in the kitchen, Peter and Katrina carrying various courses to the table whenever Peggy shouted, "Grub up!" to the accompaniment of an Austrian cowbell that she kept handy on a shelf.

Peter was complimentary about the food, telling his wife that she had excelled herself. Peggy made a face. "Katrina helped me make it, she's a sorceress in the kitchen. My cheese soufflé invariably falls flat on its face but Katrina waved a magic wand, and hey presto! Perfect soufflé! She'll make a wonderful wife for someone. After all, the way to a man's heart is through his stomach – or so they say!" At this she gave Katrina a rather defiant grin and Katrina had to smile and make some lighthearted remark in return, determined as she was by now not to let her front down.

After dinner, all three of them 'mucked in' as Belle would have put it, and the dishes were cleared away in no time. "Right, let's have a nice cosy evening," Peggy decided, "into the living room you two, I've lit the gas fire so the room should be nice and warm and there's plenty to drink in the cabinet. Peter, you do the honours, will you? Pour me a dry martini with lemonade and ice, you know the way I like it. I'm just going to check on the children – be back in a tick." She was gone for only a few minutes but had no sooner sat down than she jumped up again. "The *book*! Fancy me forgetting that. Hang on, I won't be a moment."

Peter looked at Katrina and grinned. "It's like living with an express train, never still for a minute, except in the morning when I have to kick her out of bed. Was she always like that? Or has marriage and children turned a once calm pool into a tidal wave?"

Katrina laughed. "Peggy was never one to let the grass grow under her feet. Even so, she knew how to relax and was so laid back at times she got called Dolly Daydream at school. Having kids has certainly pepped her up a bit. It could be she's got no time to daydream anymore – or perhaps it's just that she's found what she was looking for all along and doesn't need to sit back thinking about it now."

He turned from the drinks cabinet to look at her quizzically. "And you, Katie? Have you fulfilled your dreams yet? Or are you still looking?"

Katrina was relieved that she didn't have to answer that question as Peggy came steaming back just then, waving a book in mid-air, saying breathlessly, "*Look*, Peter, you'll never guess what's in this. Just take a peep inside and see for yourself."

She thrust the book under his nose and he stared in amazement at the inscription written on it. "Larry Sinclair! Where did you meet him? Was he in Inverness signing books?"

"No, silly, he was here, in this very house, this very day!"

"*Here, in our house?* But what on earth was he doing *here*?"

"He came to see Katie."

Peter swung round to Katrina. "Seeing *you*, Katie? Do you know him? Personally?"

"I should think she does," Peggy said with not a trace of contrition.

"I did know him – at least – we've known one another for years," Katrina explained in some confusion. "He was around when I came to Speyside as a kid, but after that we lost touch and I only met him again a couple of weeks ago."

"Well, well, it just goes to show, all things are possible." Peter looked again at the signature on his book and Katrina threw Peggy a silent plea to get her out of a situation which was becoming more awkward by the second.

"Scrabble!" Peggy said briskly. "Put the book away, Peter, and come and sit down. A game of scrabble is just what we all need to get our minds off everyday matters and help us relax."

Peter sighed and threw his eyes heavenward. "Relax? With scrabble? You know you always cheat, Peggy, and we usually end up arguing. I don't see anything relaxing about that." But Peggy wasn't taking no for an answer. A space had been made on the coffee table, the scrabble board was out; there was no escape for Peter or anyone else.

Peggy looked at Katrina. "I've filled bowls with crisps and nuts in the kitchen – get them, will you, Katie? Oh, and there's a Mars bar for Peter, third drawer from the top in the herb chest. I've got to put everything up high out of Fiona's reach."

"A Mars bar?" Katrina had to ask.

"Yes, of course, dear," Peggy looked surprised. "He

always has a Mars bar when we play scrabble, otherwise he'd never get the grey cells to work. There's a lot of energy in a Mars bar."

Katrina rushed to the kitchen choking with laughter. Peggy was like a tonic, one that could brighten anybody up. It had been like that in school, Peggy saying wonderfully ridiculous things in the classroom, Katrina smothering back the laughter and almost bursting in the process.

She took a deep breath. She felt better – and scrabble was just the thing *she* needed to keep her mind off Larry.

Chapter Twenty-One

KATRINA departed around ten the next morning. She had spent another restless night reliving over and over the scene with Larry, and as a result she was taut and drawn, and her fingers seemed to be all thumbs as she fumbled with the zip of her jacket.

"Are you sure you'll be all right?" Peggy asked, gazing anxiously into her friend's face. "I wish there was something I could do to help, but it's so difficult in matters of the heart."

"You have helped." Katrina gave her a grateful hug. "You've been patient and sympathetic and just being with you and the babies has taken my mind off things – oh, by the way, I've left presents for them in my room, you can put them under the tree later."

"Oh, Katie, you really shouldn't have bothered, they're far too young to know what it's all about yet," she looked pensive. "Don't you wish sometimes you could go back to childhood, when all you had to concern you was whether Santa had left the doll you longed for?"

Katrina smiled. "Unlike you I was never the dolly type, but it would be nice to go back sometimes and undo a few of the silly mistakes one makes along the way."

Peggy stroked Fiona's fair hair absently. "You're

regretting it then? Sending him away? Oh, it's none of my business, I know – yet, in a way, it *has* been, and I'm still hoping the pair of you might get together after all."

Katrina retrieved the car keys from her shoulder bag. "He'll probably be in London by now and he won't come running back here a second time – not after the things I said." She bent to drop a kiss on Fiona's plump cheek, the little girl gurgled with delight and waved a dimpled hand as Katrina opened the door. "Don't bother to come down, Pegs, it's cold and I think I hear Jamie crying. Have a good Christmas. I'll phone you and perhaps try and get back to see you before I return to London."

A few minutes later she was settled in the Mini. Peggy's hand fluttered at the window and she felt oddly sad to be going away. Peggy had been her best friend at school, and though they hadn't seen so much of each other in the intervening years they had never lost touch and when they did meet it was with the ease of two people assured of one another's trust.

In a short time she was driving through open country. If she hadn't been so overwrought she would have enjoyed the run back. It was a soft, golden day, the sky a palette of pearly greys and soft blues; the winter colours of the moors blended with the mosaic of brown and green fields stretching to the misted purple of the faraway hills.

She wasn't looking forward to facing Belle, yet, when she brought the Mini to a halt in the yard everything looked so serene and peaceful she experienced a surge of joy to be back. But when Belle didn't appear at the door to greet her, her uneasiness returned and she went indoors warily.

On the threshold she paused, her mouth falling open at sight of Jilly warming her feet by the Aga. "Surprise! Surprise!" Jilly rushed forward to enclose her friend in a bear hug.

"Jilly! How on earth did *you* get here?" gasped Katrina.

Jilly ran her fingers through bubbly curls. "I was bored, Katie," she said plaintively. "I told you I was missing you, and everyone else had invitations to stay with relatives. I felt left out so last night I hopped on a sleeper. When I got in this morning I phoned here, thinking you would be back from Peggy's and could pick me up. You weren't, so Bob came to rescue a damsel in distress. Phew! I've ridden in clapped-out bangers in my time but that old heap of his is a real vintage bone-shaker."

"You phoned from the station? That must have been rather early." Katrina was experiencing a certain amount of resentment at Jilly's intrusion. She had, after all, been the cause of yesterday's row with Larry, yet here she was, bold as brass, behaving as if nothing had happened.

"I saw no point in hanging about in the cold," Jilly spoke airily. "Anyway, aren't farmers supposed to be early birds? I was back in time for breakfast and now I'm having a rest – I'm whacked." Her big blue eyes swept critically over Katrina. "I can't say your holiday has done you much good. It's that worm, Sinclair, isn't it? I hope you aren't still seeing him. I did warn you about him – I only hope I wasn't too late."

"Yes, you did warn me," Katrina couldn't keep the bitterness out of her voice. "Don't concern yourself any more. It's finished. We had a row and he's gone back to London."

"Really?"

"Yes – oh, damn it! Don't go on about him!" Katrina frowned. "I don't really understand you, Jilly. You were anxious for me to get myself a man, yet when I did you made a thorough job of shooting him down in flames."

Jilly's eyes grew hard. "I told you, he isn't the one for you. Sinclair's a swine where women are concerned, a chauvinistic pig if ever there was one!"

"Yes, you made that clear enough." Katrina's brow creased again. "One thing puzzles me, though. Why did you never mention him to me before? You're very frank about the men in your life – so why not Larry?"

"Sinclair has a knack of making a girl feel special." Jilly's voice was icy, "You know, you think it's the real thing and you wait in hope, saying nothing – so I said nothing. Anyway, you weren't on the scene then and by the time you popped back, it was history. To tell the truth, I was as hurt as hell the way he dumped me for someone else, and didn't want it to be known that little Jilly had fallen hook, line and sinker for a bastard!"

Katrina flushed, "I know the feeling," she said faintly.

Belle appeared, looking more harassed than normal. "Katrina," she acknowledged. "I didn't hear the car, I've been rather busy upstairs." Her voice held undertones of disapproval and she looked meaningfully at Jilly's outdoor clothes strewn over the chairs.

Katrina put her hand under Belle's arm and guided her out of earshot. "Belle, I'm sorry about this," she began apologetically. "I'm as surprised as you. Jilly was the last person on earth I expected to turn up."

Belle's lips tightened. "She didn't come to fill her lungs with country air, that's for sure. It didn't take her long to get round to talking about Larry – it seems she knows him."

"Yes, yes she does – or rather, she did."

"Hmph," Belle snorted disapprovingly. "It will be interesting to see what Larry has to say about *that*." She looked round distractedly. "Where am I going to put her? The spare room has a drip above the bed and it's soaked. I told Bob about the slates, but he's always so busy . . ."

"Belle, calm down, it's not like you to get upset. The answer is simple. We'll put a mattress in my room and Jilly can have my bed. She *has* been good to me, Belle, and I really don't mind." Inwardly she groaned at the chaos Jilly would create in her room, but she was rewarded by the sight of Belle's brow clearing. "By the way, Belle," she said awkwardly, "I'm sorry I put you in such a spot over Larry."

"Oh, Katrina, it's me who ought to apologise for telling him where you were," she studied Katrina's pale face anxiously. "He was so keen to see you, I just couldn't hold out on him."

"Perhaps it's as well. There were things that had to be said and now we both know where we stand."

"Really? And where exactly is that?"

Katrina sighed. "Belle, it's over. It never really began actually, and I don't want to say any more on the subject."

"He's gone then?" Belle's tones were bleak. "What about the party?"

Katrina hugged her affectionately. "There's absolutely no reason why we shouldn't have it. Jilly will enjoy it and I'm looking forward to it as well."

The party was the last thing on her mind, but somehow she managed to get through the next two days with every appearance of enjoyment. Jilly's presence certainly helped, though she was so untidy about the house that even Belle was moved to complain, and Katrina spent her time clearing up piles of clothes which littered the bedroom floor.

On Christmas Day, Bob went to fetch Aunt Annie to bring her back to Balgower for dinner. Aunt Annie had excelled herself as far as her appearance went. She was wearing a blue twinset and a tweed skirt, but it was her hat which made her stand out again. This time a lilac 'flying saucer' as Bob called it later; its brim decorated with large, felt orchids and a feather that Belle claimed must have come straight off a peacock's backside, so bright and fresh were the colours. Jilly couldn't take her eyes off it, and Aunt Annie, noticing the girl's eyes on her, barked out, "What's the matter, lass? Don't they have peacocks in London?"

"Er – no, not exactly, at least, I don't think so," Jilly stuttered, for once lost for a smart reply. "Pigeons, yes, starlings too, but, no, I don't think I've ever seen a peacock in the streets of London."

Aunt Annie gave a devilish smile. "Good thing too, they're noisy brutes, they'd wake you up in the morning and no mistake. A hat's the best place for them; they can't make much noise on a hat." She paused with a Brussels sprout half-way to her mouth, "Come to think of it, I've never seen a peacock either. Oh, I've heard them all right, screeching like ghosts through the woods in the gentry estates, and that was enough for me. Jeemie used to bring the feathers home though, he was a gamekeeper up at the big house over by Insh and had access to all sorts of game and ornamental birds, feathers and all."

Jilly had never met anyone quite like Aunt Annie. She was totally fascinated by her and the stories she told afterwards when they were all seated round the fire drinking sherry and eating rum truffles. "Is she *real*?" she asked Katrina later. "I mean, she's absolutely brilliant. I wish I could have her at one of my parties. She'd knock 'em dead with her hats and her yarns."

"Oh, she's real, all right, known as a character in these parts. She pretends to be all fangs and claws but in her own way she's as soft as putty, and she certainly helped me to forget myself just when I most needed it."

"Hmm, Larry again?" Jilly drawled as she lay on the bed eating an apple.

"Not any more," Katrina replied evenly, as she automatically picked up a pair of Jilly's jeans from the floor and placed them over the back of a chair.

On the eve of the Boxing Day party Katrina had a bath and went into her room to get ready. Jilly was sprawled on the bed polishing her nails. She was already dressed, vivacious-looking in the red dress she'd borrowed from Katrina before she left London.

Katrina had brought only two dresses with her and she decided on the least formal, a white silk shift which felt lovely and cool against her skin. Rather listlessly she applied mascara and a touch of lipstick, and as she ran a comb through her hair she gazed broodingly at her reflection, wondering if her pallor had something to do with the way the light was shining, or if it was a result of too many sleepless nights. She fingered the gold chain lying on the dressing table, undecided whether to wear it. Some of the magic of that lovely evening at River Cottage came back to her and dreamily, as if of their own volition, her hands reached out to pick up the chain and clasp it round her neck.

Jilly lifted her head to gaze at her friend consideringly, "Hmm, not bad, you don't look a hundred per cent though. Still thinking of *him*, aren't you? Forget him, obviously he's flushed you out of his system good and proper. If he'd thought anything at all of you he wouldn't have given up so easily. There's other fish, Katie, and who knows, if we're lucky we might just bait a couple at this party – no harm in having a giggle anyway."

The sitting room was welcoming and cosy with the lights of the Christmas tree splashing colourful hues over the red carpet and an amber glow from two lamps adding warmth. Bob had removed the electric fire from the grate, and a coal fire now took its place, adding to the friendly atmosphere. A cold buffet had been laid out in the dining room next door and the table was laden with vol-au-vents, hors-d'œuvre, piles of sandwiches and bowls of ham and turkey salad, all of which Katrina had helped to prepare earlier in the day.

People were still at the standing about stage, sipping rather self-consciously at drinks and making desultory conversation, and Bob, having carried out introductions, retired to a corner where a group of ruddy-faced men were having a confab about hill sheep.

Katrina didn't recognise many of the faces around her, but the arrival of Winnie MacAuley and her husband soon fixed that. Winnie was magnificent in her party wear and as soon as she spotted Katrina she crossed the room towards her like a ship in full sail, while her husband made good his escape by joining Bob and his cronies in the corner.

"Katrina," Winnie gushed, extending her hand graciously. "How nice to see you again. I was asking Belle only the other day how you and Larry were getting on. Still hanging on to him, I hope? Last time we spoke you weren't too sure if you and he would meet up again."

Katrina opened her mouth and shut it again, not quite knowing how to handle someone as loud as Winnie, but she was saved by the bell, as it were, when Joe the Post suddenly appeared in front of her to introduce her to his wife, a pleasant little woman with a kindly smile and, most importantly for Katrina just then, a *quiet* voice.

Belle, who was taking her hostess duties seriously, came over and offered the tray to Katrina, who chose a glass of dry martini. "Take something stronger," said Belle persuasively. "It is Christmas after all." Rashly, Katrina decided on gin and tonic. Let your hair down, she told herself flippantly, even though she felt a touch of remorse. Bob and Belle had thrown this party for her sake and she felt guilty because it had been meant for Larry, too. Belle hadn't mentioned his name again yet Katrina knew only too well what she was thinking.

She immersed herself in helping to dispense drinks. The atmosphere was perceptibly mellower than it had been. Katrina noticed that several fiddles and an accordian had been left in the hall and she guessed there would be a period of warming up before a real Highland element got into full swing.

Jilly was in sparkling form, conversing with a black-bearded, kilted young man who was gazing at her as if he could eat her.

Jacky, evading Elaine for a moment, came over to Katrina and told her she was looking lovely and that he hoped she would dance with him later. "You'll have to arrange that with Elaine's blessing," she laughed. "I'd hate to think I was causing trouble between the two of you, but I'd love a dance with you as long as it's okay with her."

Some of the other men, having lost their initial shyness, were in the mood to be sociable and made it their business to speak to Katrina, though she was careful to flit from one to the other as she had no desire to allow herself to get pinned down by anyone – not even by a big, red-haired kiltie, whose marvellous physique had already caused quite a stir among the women in the gathering.

"Lighten up, Katrina," Jilly mouthed in passing. "There are one or two passable men here and it wouldn't do you any harm to at least talk to them – unless, of course, you're still thinking Larry might turn up and carry you off to his lair in the hills."

Katrina didn't deign to answer this and turned away,

wishing Jilly wouldn't keep bringing up the subject of Larry when she was trying so hard to keep her mind away from him – and the magic they'd shared so briefly at River Cottage.

Chapter Twenty-Two

BY ten o'clock the party was well under way. The fiddles had tuned up and strains of a waltz filled the room. Katrina, feeling only in the mood to spectate, slipped over to the door as the dancers drifted by. She was unable to suppress a pang of emotion. The night could have been so different – if only . . .

She jumped, and her heart hammered into her throat. Strong hands had seized her from behind and in her fright she stumbled and found herself supported by Larry. Without a word he guided her onto the floor, his hold on her so tight she could hardly breathe, let alone break away. "Why are you here?" she demanded when she had gathered sufficient breath to speak.

"Why not?" his voice was cool. "I was invited."

"W-when?"

"The day I came here looking for you."

"But – but Belle thought – I thought you were in London?"

"So, you were all wrong." The words held a familiar mockery and she coloured. The firm, sensuous line of his mouth was just inches from her own and his hands moved to her hips to pull her in closer.

"I don't know why you're doing this," she breathed shakily.

In answer his lips brushed her ear and she got the distinct impression he was deliberately tormenting her. "You're tense," he told her lightly. "Calm down. You and I have a few things to thrash out. You'll need your strength for that."

"Larry," she whispered weakly, "we've been through all this."

"We haven't started yet," he said patiently and her senses spun as she wondered what he meant. She felt him stiffen suddenly, and abruptly he let her go. "Excuse me," his voice was distant, "I've just spotted someone I know."

She watched him walk casually over to where Jilly was in animated conversation with the black-bearded young man. Larry said something to him and, rather unwillingly, he went away to replenish his glass. Katrina saw the flush spreading over Jilly's face and the brightness of her eyes as she gazed up at Larry.

Katrina turned blindly away, barely able to stem the tears clouding her vision, so that she all but stumbled into the quiet haven of the kitchen. 'You've had one drink too many, my girl,' she told herself, and pressed her fist to her lips to stem hysterical laughter which bubbled in her throat. She stood with her back to the door, hearing the music and the laughter on the other side, seeing again the look on Jilly's face at the sight of Larry.

Was that why she had come to Scotland? In the hope of meeting him? She had obviously fallen for him in a big way long before Katrina ever came on the scene. All that business about hating him was perhaps just a cover for how she still felt, and in her anxiety to win him back she had spilled out a lot of malicious gossip to Katrina in order to put her off. *And she'd succeeded!* Katrina shook her head as if to clear it. She had to face the fact that Jilly might have betrayed her and she felt sick . . .

The door opened suddenly and violently, almost throwing her off balance. Larry strode in, closing the door firmly behind him.

"Right, Katie, I want you to listen to me and listen good," he told her harshly, the hard blue of his eyes piercing into her authoritatively. She stood in the middle of the room, looking at him with eyes dark with unhappiness. "Sit down, Katie," his voice was softer. "What I have to say might take a while." She obeyed, simply because she doubted if her shaking legs would have supported her a minute longer. He grabbed a high-backed kitchen chair and, pulling it over beside her, straddled it, his arms folded over the back. "I've just spent Christmas with your friend Peggy and her husband," he told her conversationally.

"With Peggy?" she gasped.

"Yes, probably the best friend you've got. She's a great girl and Peter's a nice guy; genuine people, both. Peggy invited me when she asked for my signature in Peter's book. I got there on the evening of the day you left – in time for drinks with Peter and a nice cosy chat with Peggy. She told me you'd talked to our not-so-dumb blonde back there. Tell me what the little vixen had to say, Katie, I've got a right to know exactly what's been said behind my back?"

In a low voice Katrina repeated the conversation she'd had with Jilly on the phone and when she finally came to a faltering halt Larry's face was white under his tan. "You were really taken in by the treacherous bitch, weren't you? Oh, she probably hit on a few truths – I've loved and left a few, what man of my age hasn't? I told you I was no plaster saint. As for going to bed with her—" his mouth quirked sarcastically. "She's got more imagination than I gave her credit for – I wouldn't touch her with a ten foot pole."

Katrina was staring at him. "But – you do *know* her, Larry. You can't deny that."

He laughed shortly. "Yes, I know her, I met her at some party or other. She was with Carrington – when you mentioned his name that day at the Ptarmigan it only vaguely clicked. But that evening at the cottage, when you spoke of Jilly Watson, I put two and two together. He threw you over for her, Katie, but she soon tired of him; she was hunting for bigger game, and she set her sights on me . . ."

"Paul – and – *Jilly*," Katrina squeezed the words out, remembering something Jilly had said about Paul being a dead loss as a man – how could she have known that, unless . . .

Larry glanced at her white face and went out of the room, returning with a glass of brandy which he pushed into her trembling hands, standing over her while she gulped it down. "Do you want me to go on?" he asked and she nodded wordlessly. "Normally I like pretty little blondes," he stated flatly, "but, as I've already explained, I don't like being chased, especially by an obvious gold-digger. Her greedy claws showed from the start and I had nothing to do with her. That incensed her and she's hated me ever since – a good example of a woman scorned, if you like. She was enraged when she thought you were going to get something she couldn't, and she set out to spoil it for you—" his lip curled. "The spiteful little darling came down here to make sure she'd succeeded. And of course, she was getting back at me – killing two birds with one stone."

"But – she was taking a risk, wasn't she?" Katrina said in puzzlement. "Coming up here? What if you'd still been here – or rather, what if you and I had still been, still been—"

"She struck while the iron was hot." Larry's voice was harsh. "She knew what kind of girl you were and how wary you were after your experiences with Carrington. And she might have got away with it if Peggy hadn't intervened. Believe me, after the things you said, I was all for heading back south – I don't take kindly to being made a fool of." He glanced at Katrina's face and his eyes narrowed contemplatively as he added, "Anyway, I'm here, and Jilly almost fainted when she saw me just now."

Katrina lowered her head and her voice quavered when she said, "I – at the moment I can't think straight. I don't know what I feel for Jilly . . . I can't hate her despite everything. She's been good to me and helped me when I needed help."

"Salving her conscience," he said contemptuously. "You don't need friends like Jilly." He stood up and, pulling something from his pocket, laid it on the table. "I bought this in London. Even if you won't accept it for what it is, keep it anyway to remember me by. It's

211

up to you now, Katie. I've done my share of the running – you know where to find me if you want me."

He went quickly away, the door clicking behind him. Through a wavering mist she stared at the small domed box on the table before picking it up to open it with trembling hands. The brilliance of the sapphire and diamond engagement ring caught the light and dazzled her. The stones were set into a slender white gold band and she held her breath as she slipped it on. It was almost a perfect fit and she sat for a long, long time gazing at it.

"Larry," she whispered at last, and the feeling that swelled in her heart was one of love. Jumping up she went to seek out Belle to explain she was going to bed as she intended to get up early. "I don't want you to think I'm not enjoying the party," she said rather breathlessly. "It's just that, well – I want to be alone to think."

Belle gazed into her glowing face. "Katrina, what's happened?" she demanded. "I saw Larry and I wanted to speak to him, but it would seem he's gone."

"Oh Belle, forgive him, forgive me if I seem rude but—" she held up her finger, "—to be truthful I don't know whether I'm coming or going. Larry and I are engaged – I'm going to tell him tomorrow."

Belle's face was a study of delight and bemusement. "Going to tell him? But, surely he knows?"

Katrina hugged her. "I'll explain everything later. Can I borrow your car in the morning?"

"Of course you can," Belle smiled, waltzing Katrina round. "You can borrow anything you like! It's wonderful news."

"Don't tell anyone just yet, oh—" Katrina paused in

212

dismay. "I forgot – I *completely* forgot! With everything that's been on my mind I . . ."

"Forgot what?" Belle shook her head.

"Larry's present. I wanted to see him as early as possible tomorrow, but now I'll have to go to Aviemore first – and the shop might not be open—"

Belle was beaming. She bustled away and returned holding a wrapped package. "I took it upon myself to collect it. With you staying at Peggy's, I'd an idea you mightn't manage to get it yourself."

"Belle, you're – well you're a darling! Thank you," Katrina said huskily and turning, she slipped quickly upstairs. She undressed and got into the camp-bed Bob had brought down from the attic when she'd given up her own bed to Jilly.

Jilly hadn't yet come up and she was glad as she didn't want to speak to her. Later perhaps, but at the moment her mind was too taken up with other matters. She lay awake, gazing up at the ceiling, not expecting to sleep, hearing the sounds of merriment from downstairs, thinking, wondering, gradually drifting off . . .

She woke early. Jilly was sound asleep, her blonde head tousled on her pillows. Katrina felt no resentment towards her. In a strange way Jilly had done her a favour by bringing matters to a head.

Slipping out of bed she gathered together fresh underwear, jeans, and a warm sweater, and stole from the room to the bathroom to shower and dress. No one was about, not even Bob, who rarely stayed in bed in the morning. She made tea and sat down at the Aga to drink it, hardly able to take her eyes off the sparkling ring on her finger.

213

It was tangible proof that Larry's feelings towards her were more than just a passing fancy – proof that he might even – love her.

She seemed to float outside. It was a bright, clean morning with a fresh wind blowing down from the hills and she raised her face to the sky, savouring each sight and sound as if for the first time. Ten minutes later she was guiding the Mini along the winding track to River Cottage and it seemed she was traversing a path she'd known and loved for a long time. A thin spiral of smoke rose from the chimneys of the house.

She climbed out of the car, feeling suddenly apprehensive, but he was at the door, and as she walked towards him she saw the joy lighting his face. Without hesitation she went to him to say steadily, "I'm sorry for ever having doubted you, my darling, and for being afraid to admit that I loved you."

He was staring at her in disbelief. "Katie," he murmured huskily and his arms went round her, pulling her in so close she could feel the thudding of his heart. He drew her inside to the den where the logs were crackling in the grate and he paused with her in the middle of the room to cup her face in his hands and kiss her deeply. "Katie, Katie," he said softly, "I've waited a long time for this moment but I knew you wouldn't come to me till the ghost of Carrington was laid to rest, once and for all. I could have told you about him and Jilly that night at the cottage but I couldn't hurt you – not even when I thought I was losing you—" He laughed, "I suppose you could say good came out of bad – Jilly set the ball rolling by blabbing her mouth off to you, and Peggy set both of us on the right tracks in her own inimitable way."

"But – when the book was finished, why did you go away without a word? Without even leaving a phone number?"

He raked his fingers through his hair and smiled at her in some bemusement. "Because I didn't know what was happening to me. I've never truly loved a woman till I met you. It was rather a strange experience – to feel so involved. I could hardly think straight. I needed to be completely cut off from you to get everything into perspective. I couldn't get back quick enough, only to find you didn't want to see me. I went haywire."

"I know, you terrified me."

"I know, I even frightened myself. I've always been in control of my feelings . . ." he laughed, "—until a little witch came along and completely bowled me over." A frown darkened his brow. "I still can't understand why you wouldn't tell me straightaway the things Jilly spat at you. Not schoolgirl honour, surely?"

"Of course not," she protested, "I – well, to be honest, you sounded just like Paul and I simply couldn't face anything like that again. Also – this might sound silly, but I-I hated the idea of you thinking that I was – well – too available—"

"Available!" his lips twitched. "Little witch. The thing I love most about you is your innocence." He sat down and pulled her onto his knee. 'How would you like to become my permanent right hand man?"

"You-you mean . . . ?"

"I mean, I want us to be married right away. We'll spend a short time at my London pad while you sort out your affairs, then we'll fly to some remote spot in the world for our honeymoon. Agreeable?"

"It sounds wonderful. I can't believe it's all happening to me."

He held her face in his hands and looked seriously into her eyes. "Katie, I've been a bit of a wanderer, but lately I've had the urge to settle somewhere. You and I both have roots here. Would it upset you very much to leave the city and come back to live in Scotland? It's not as if you'd be buried, we would have to travel a lot to get colour for my books . . ."

"Larry!" she gave a shout of joy and threw her arms round his neck, smothering any further words in a kiss which gave him his answer. When they eventually came back to reality she said breathlessly, "I have things to do. I want to phone Peggy and I think we ought to go and tell Belle all our news."

Flakes of snow were falling as they made their way outside. "You don't think we should just wait and get snowed up?" he suggested with a grin.

"I think we ought to wait till we're married," she said firmly, and ran laughing to the car.

Belle was thrilled when she heard their plans. "I knew, of course, it would come right in the end," she beamed, her lively eyes flashing. "You were made for one another – right from the time you played together as children."

Larry tugged playfully at Katrina's hair. "I never played with this freckled witch – I fought with her."

"Yes, and see where it got you," Belle told him sternly, and winked at Katrina. "I always did say the best things are worth fighting for."

Katrina glanced round the kitchen in puzzlement. "Where is Bob by the way – and Jilly?"

"She rose soon after you left and packed her case," nodded Belle, adding innocently, "I think she was a bit bored with the country. Bob's away with her to the station. She said to tell you goodbye . . ." Belle glanced absently at the trayloads of glasses waiting beside the sink to be washed. "I was wondering if we ought to have the New Year party early – tomorrow night for instance. We could make it a double celebration: an engagement party and a Hogmanay party combined. The only thing is, I haven't recovered yet from last night. I keep forgetting where I put things."

Larry laughed and held up his wrist, "Get yourself one of these, Belle, at least you'll always remember your own name. This girl—" he slipped his arm round Katrina's waist, "—has got the shackles on me already. I'll never be able to escape now."

"Do you want to?" she said lightly.

He bent his head and kissed her. "I shouldn't think so. I've never been married to a witch before; I'm looking forward to the novelty."

Belle looked at them standing with their arms round one another, and with a smile she went to put her apron on.